ALL THAT WAITS
IN THE NIGHT

ALSO BY J. PATRICK LEMARR

The Willing, The Wounded, and The Wizard (a novella)
The Christmas Cabin
Shadow Plays: 15 Stories of Darkness and Light
A Secret Sin, A Silent Sea (Tales of the Evermore Book Two)
The Witches of Greyfolk (Tales of the Evermore Book One)
Underneath
I Am a Broken House

ALL THAT WAITS IN THE NIGHT

A HORROR EVENT

Published in the United States by Write Crowd Publishing.

Paperback ISBN 978-0-9838337-4-1
Hardcover ISBN 978-1-958476-98-7

WRITE CROWD PUBLISHING
WWW.WRITECROWDPUBLISHING.COM

FOR B

ALL THAT WAITS IN THE NIGHT

TABLE OF CONTENTS::

"CIVILIZATION IS HIDEOUSLY FRAGILE...THERE'S NOT MUCH BETWEEN US AND THE HORRORS UNDERNEATH, JUST ABOUT A COAT OF VARNISH."

C.P. SNOW

PREFACE

The stories you are about to read were my attempt to cheat. Serialized storytelling a few thousand words at a time was a challenge I thought would be exciting…especially for a new digital platform which, for all I knew, could've been the "next big thing in publishing." As I thought about what sort of horror story I would write for it, however, I found I had far too many ideas and none of them required the length of a serialized novel. Whatever would I do? Cheat. That's what.

I wrote "The Eyes and Corrine Mathers" in one sitting the morning after it first infiltrated my brain. Originally known simply as "The Eyes," it seemed to be a teaser for a larger tale. The Drew Barrymore scene of my Scream. The end of a previous story as a new one begins…à la the James Bond movies. It was then I settled on the cheat. I would use the serialized platform to publish short stories, which would eventually (if the reader stuck with me) reveal a larger tale happening behind them all.

Unfortunately, the "next big thing in publishing" proved to be dead on arrival, so my duplicitous ploy went virtually unnoticed. To make matters worse, I was contractually bound to not publish these tales elsewhere until a certain amount of time had passed. I could do nothing but wait. Oh, and *move across the country.*

Once these stories were mine to release into the world in print form, I considered the order in which they would appear. On a serialized digital platform, I understood some readers might only read a chapter or two and never grasp the larger story. I designed the release order with that in mind. Multiple part stories released in close enough proximity to allow readers to reach the rest of the story quickly, even if it weakened the experience of the overarching plot.

Now, however, I can guarantee that you have complete access to the whole shebang without having to buy into it piece by piece. I've restructured the order of stories to (hopefully) bolster the overall reading experience and give you the most literary bang for your hard-to-come-by buck. I even added a 13th story to bring a bit more resolution and do some world-building for stories to come.

The result now rests in your capable hands. Love it. Hate it. Either way, review it! (Pretty please.) I'm biased, of course, but I believe it's a fun ride through the darkest corners of my imagination…one I hope leaves you more appreciative of the light.

J. Patrick Lemarr

CHAPTER 1/
THE EYES AND CORRINE MATHERS

The drive up the Northern California hillside to 1837 Macklemore Avenue wound like a serpent through the sycamores and cottonwoods, many of which stood long before the construction of the half-dozen modern architectural behemoths housing their elite residents. While paved, the road was a single lane affair, closed to thru traffic and a bit of a roller coaster ride for those less familiar with its bends, curves, and steep inclines.

On that cool autumn night in 2007, still carrying the slightest buzz from her third cocktail, Corrine Mathers thought the drive home felt particularly fraught with danger. For Sean Mathers, sober and madly in love with his Westminster blue Jaguar XK, it seemed a bit like flying. The sharp curves of macadam submitted to his skillful handling and the car's smooth responses. He felt a tinge of sadness as he turned off the road onto his own driveway. It had been a fine day and a better night.

"You drive too fast," Corrine said with a playful pout as he pulled into the garage.

And you drink too much," he teased. "The designated

driver has to make his own fun."

"*I* could make you some fun," she replied, kissing his neck.

"Is that a promise?"

"Definitely. I just need to make a grocery list for Sandra and then I'll be up."

"Being up is *my* part of the equation, dear," he said with a wink. "Take your time with the grocery list. I'm going for a quick spin through the shower."

"And then the fun?"

"If that last Negroni didn't make you too sleepy, it's on."

After tapping the button to lower the garage door, Sean hopped out of the car and jogged around to the passenger door where he helped his wife exit.

"Honestly, Sean," she grumbled. "I'm a little light in my Louboutins, but I hardly need you to schlepp me inside."

"No one is schlepping," he insisted, keeping her locked to his hip as they walked. "I just like holding you close to me."

"As lies go, that's a sweet one." She kissed his cheek and added, "Okay, so maybe I'm a lightweight."

"We were celebrating. No one's judging."

"I just hope I don't pay for it tomorrow. I've got brunch with your mother."

"Ouch," he said with a wince, escorting her through the

door into the mudroom. "Don't let her steamroller you, Corrine. She's been on a tear lately. I can't tell you how many voice messages I have from Selina complaining about Mom's micromanaging."

Selina, Sean's older sister, lived half a world away and seldom came back to the states. Her mother's interference, it seemed, had not lessened with distance.

"Your sister would holler if she was hung with a new rope," Corrine mused, kicking off her shoes.

"Your native Texan always comes out when you've been drinking," he said, kissing her forehead before setting the house alarm. "Make your list. I'll shower."

"Keep your motor running," she said, shuffling toward the kitchen. "I'll be up in two shakes—"

"—of a lamb's tail," he finished. "I know."

It took no more than ten minutes for Corrine Mathers to peruse the pantry and jot down her grocery list for Sandra Contreras, a culinary student she employed as a personal chef. It took another two minutes to carefully ascend the staircase and make her way to the master suite, unbuttoning her blouse as she walked.

As she pushed her way through the double doors of the master bedroom, she stopped to admire the intricate carvings on their surface. She had paid a small fortune to import the doors from Bangladesh, but they brought her great joy. They were among very few furnishings in the home that stood out among the house's otherwise sleek and modern aesthetic. To her, those strong teak doors made their bedroom seem like a refuge from the world outside.

She inhaled deeply and smiled. The scent of her husband's body wash still clung to the steam in the air. She had hoped to find him in the bedroom still covered in droplets with a towel wrapped around his waist...a towel she would have the pleasure of removing herself. Instead, she found the room empty.

"Sean?"

The shower was no longer running, but she ventured into the en suite anyway. Though the steam hindered her vision, the bathroom was clearly empty. Sean's razor sat perched near his sink as if he had intended to shave and then thought better of it.

"I was looking to get laid by a married man," she said loudly, trying to ignore the familiar twinge of dread in the pit of her stomach. "I was told this was the place, but—"

She smiled, suddenly remembering the business proposal he had mentioned at dinner.

'Silly boy had a brainstorm in the shower and made a naked dash to his office,' she thought, amused by the mental image.

Corrine Mathers left her blouse at the foot of the bed and

shimmied out of her $400 skirt, making her way down the hall in nothing but the lingerie she had bought for the evening's celebration.

"If I have to hunt all over this house for you, Sean Mathers," she called, "my engine might overheat. Or is that what you're hoping for?"

The office was empty. The air inside seemed stale.

"Sean?"

There was a note of worry in the way she called his name. She didn't care for it.

"Damn it, Sean! Stop playing games!" she shouted, stepping back into the hallway. "I'm too drunk for this sh–"

She stopped when she noticed that the door to the guest room was slightly ajar. It usually remained closed unless they expected overnight company.

"Sean?"

Every step toward the room tied a new knot in her gut. Her skin, pleasantly warm moments earlier, was now gooseflesh, cold and pale.

"Did we move the party to the guest room?" she managed, denying the urge to panic. Her arm froze in place as she reached for the knob.

She told herself she was being ridiculous. They were safe at home. The alarm was set. Sean was just playing games. It wasn't the Eyes. Not again. She hadn't seen them since...

well, in an awfully long time. And all the best psychiatrists had assured her and her mother that the experience she had described was nothing more than a child's imagination struggling to make sense of a tragedy.

But Corrine remembered how she felt when she saw those Eyes as a child: the chill in her blood, the ache in her bones, and the panic racing up her spine. It was the exact same feeling she had with one hand on the guest room door.

Through the slight opening, she saw nothing but darkness.

"Sean? Babe?"

She fought past her panic and nudged the door open. Beyond the frame, she could see nothing...as if all light had been chased from the room. She stood in the doorway and reached to her right with a trembling hand, groping in the void for the light switch. Once she found it, she hesitated.

"I don't believe in you," Corinne said aloud. "You aren't here. You weren't there *then*, either. You were just a figment of a broken-hearted girl's imagination."

She flipped the switch. Nothing happened, except...*something* did. Near the center of the room, there was movement.

"I don't believe in you," she said again, holding onto the door frame as her knees turned to jelly.

The Eyes peered back at her, as crimson as her father's blood had once been, spilling out onto the hay.

"Yes," something growled. "You do."

The Eyes were gone by the time the lights in the room flickered back on, revealing her dear, ruined Sean...his once handsome face distorted by terror into a gruesome death mask. His insides no longer in their place.

CHAPTER 2/
LAYOVER

Parker Lennox was not a fan of air travel. She never had been. Something about the notion of strapping herself into a hollow metal tube packed with people, possessions, and potentially explosive fuel never sat well with her. And, since her job had seldom required it, it had not become as mundane to her as it tended to with most business travelers. No, for Parker, flying was a rarity…like an honest politician or a genuine activist. When she had to fly, she did. She was a grown woman and mother of two after all. She always did whatever was necessary. But she didn't have to like it.

This particular flight had her nerves more threadbare than usual because she wasn't flying alone. Her toddler, Seth, was buckled tightly into the seat next to her, happily munching on the Honey Nut Cheerios she had packed in his favorite snack cup, while 4-month-old baby Soleil sat in her lap. The altitude had made the infant cranky, though the pacifier had helped prevent a wail sure to disturb the entire cabin.

In San Francisco, they would be picked up at the airport by Parker's mother, Justine, and her latest husband, Kyle, whom Justine hoped was 'the charm' after her previous duo of failed marriage attempts.

Before San Fran, however, came a short layover in Denver where, loaded down with two children and assorted carry-ons, Parker would have to find her way through an unfamiliar airport to a different terminal and plane via which she would continue her journey to the Golden State. She was wearing a hole in her bottom lip from biting on it with worry. Her anxiety wasn't helped by the knowledge yet another take-off was ahead of her.

"Could I get you anything, ma'am?" a steward with a kind face asked.

"I'd want a drink if I didn't have to cart these two through the airport in Denver," she admitted. "Maybe just some ginger ale?"

"Of course," he said, pouring her beverage. "And try not to worry. They have passenger carts you can hop aboard so you don't have to haul your things to the next gate. If there's not one waiting when we deplane, an agent at the gate desk can call one for you."

"Thank you so much," Parker said, offering a kind smile. "That's one less worry."

"You're very welcome," he replied, handing her the small cup of golden soda. "Your children are quite well behaved."

"Um, thanks? Please, don't jinx it, though. We still have a way to go."

"I'm sure they'll be fine." He tugged the beverage cart up to the next row of seats. "Good luck with the rest of your journey."

Parker nodded her thanks and noticed that young Seth had dozed off with a piece of cereal still clinched tightly between two fingers. She looked down and saw that the baby was also asleep.

'Not a bad plan,' she thought, pulling Soleil up to her shoulder and holding her close. 'Momma could use a catnap, too.'

She allowed herself to doze but it was an anxious sleep filled with dreams of invasive tendrils worming their way into her mind. She attempted to run. To fight. But there wasn't enough time. There was never enough time.

When she awoke, the baby was restless in her arms, turning her head back and forth and crying around her pacifier.

"Easy, sweety," Parker said, bringing the child's face to hers. "Momma's got you. You're just hungry."

"Momma, Momma," Seth said, a hint of worry in his squeaky little voice. "Why is baby Sully crying?"

'Sully' was the closest the young boy could get to saying his little sister's name so Parker and her husband, Matt, had decided not to correct him.

"Soleil is just upset because she's hungry, sweetheart. Just like daddy gets when he doesn't have his coffee."

"Coffee is a grow'up drink," Seth reminded. "It's not for kids."

"That's right. Not for kids."

She took the pacifier from the baby's mouth and handed it the toddler.

"Hold Soleil's binky for me while I get her bottle." She reached down to rummage through the diaper bag. "Once we get some milk in her she'll be happy as a—"

It was the stillness of the air that first gave Parker pause, followed by a sour smell that slowly settled into her taste buds. Had it been the only clue that something had gone wrong, she might have ignored it. Written the feeling off as a touch of air sickness and nothing more. But the loud droning of the engine had ceased, and in that moment, distracted by her sudden nausea, she realized it had been replaced with a quiet tension…as if the world was holding its breath.

"Momma," Seth said before she had a chance to sit up, "he looks funny."

Still bent over, she turned to find the 3-year-old pointing at the row of seats across from him. She had taken note of the man seated there when they had boarded the plane. He was middle-aged with salt and pepper hair and a polite smile. As the sole occupant of that row, he had taken the center seat to have more freedom of movement. Now, where he had been, sat…something else.

Parker knew that surrendering to the impulse to scream in

terror would serve only to frighten her children, so she swallowed her dread and focused on processing the sight before her. It still had the shape of a man but looked discolored and shriveled, a shell of brittle, desiccated flesh encasing an all-too-human skeleton that might crumble to dust with no more force than a single breath could muster. Despite its withered appearance, she was certain it had once been the man with the salt and pepper hair who was now very, very dead.

She sat up sharply and took in the contents of the entire plane ahead of her. Everywhere she looked, it was the same: withered husks where the passengers had been. She turned to glance behind her, and the story repeated itself. Her next thought was to look out the window to her left. It was impossibly bright outside, and dust whipped around the plane disrupting her view. The only thing clear to her in that moment was that they were no longer in the air. They had landed *somewhere*.

"Hello?" she called, her voice echoing through the cabin.

"Hi!" Seth offered.

She afforded him a weak smile.

"Sweetheart," she told the boy, "Momma needs you to do her a *big boy* favor. Can you do that?"

"I'm a big boy," he insisted.

"I know you are. And such a good big brother for Soleil. Can you hold her for a minute while Momma goes to check on something?"

"I hold Sully when I kiss her g'night," he reminded her. "She likes when I hold her, Momma. And when I kiss on her nose."

"I know she does, baby. But she's a little wiggly right now because she's hungry, so hold her tight but not so tight you hurt her, okay?"

"Okay, Momma."

"And stay in your seat," she added, unbuckling herself. "Momma will come right back for you."

"So we can see Gran'ma," Seth said, his hopeful smile breaking her heart.

She tucked the baby into him and put the pacifier back in her mouth.

"Just hold her, Seth. Momma will be right back."

She reluctantly stepped away from her children and worked her way up the aisle past row after row of mummified dead. Beyond the partition that separated coach from first-class, she found more corpses. At the cockpit door, she pounded loudly but heard no movement. There wasn't a man or woman left alive to help her, or talk her down from the tower of anxiety that loomed taller by the second.

She and her babies were alone on a plane full of the dead.

Parker's mind raced with too many questions, fueled by the panic rampaging through her body. Something fatal had clearly happened to everyone on that plane, so why weren't she and her children affected? Nothing about the aircraft nor the state of the bodies suggested a struggle. There seemed to be no fight for survival. Had whatever killed them done its work with such speed they hadn't had time to react? That seemed implausible to the young mother because the jet was no longer in the air. If the pilots and passengers had died mid-flight, the plane would've crashed, and Parker and her children would never have awakened from their nap. If they had touched down first, airport personnel would surely have come in with sirens blaring, concerned about an impromptu landing and moving quickly to evacuate the passengers. None of it made sense.

She retrieved her cell phone from her pocket and dialed 911. The screen flashed that it found no service. She switched on the device's Wi-Fi connectivity but saw nothing to link to.

"Momma!" Seth cried. "Momma, hurry!"

At the sound of her son's voice, all other concerns fled Parker's mind as she bolted back down the aisle to row 27, where she had left him cradling baby Soleil. As she approached, she could see that he was still holding the girl tightly to his body.

"What is it, sweety?"

"Sully is stinky."

"Soleil is—"

"I think she went poopy," the boy said, making a face that,

in any other situation, would have been adorable.

"Okay, Seth. Momma can take care of the diaper," she said, retrieving Soleil from his lap. "Unbuckle and scooch over, honey, so Momma has room to change her."

The boy did as he was asked, scooting over to the window seat and peering out into the blinding light beyond.

As she changed the baby, Parker formulated a plan for getting the three of them off the plane.

"Seth, once Momma is done changing the baby, we're going to play a game."

"Noggin?" the boy asked hopefully.

"No, sweety, this is a *new* game. It's sort of like follow the leader—"

"We play that at daycare!"

"I know," she replied, securing a fresh diaper on her squirming, still hungry daughter. "But, for this game, you have to keep your eyes closed tightly and hold my hand. I'll lead you all the way to the door of the plane and outside. If you make it the whole way without opening your eyes, you win the game. But if you open them…or I *trick* you into opening them…you *lose* the game."

"I can keep my eyes closed," he said, shutting his baby blues as proof.

"Not yet, baby. The game hasn't started yet."

She finished snapping Soleil's onesie back together and put the soiled diaper in the disposable zipper pouch she kept in her bag for such occasions. She lifted the baby to her hip and hooked the diaper bag in the crook of her elbow.

"Okay, Seth, are you ready to start our game?"

"Yes, Momma. I'm gonna win and you're gonna buy me an ice cream for being the winner. It's ice cream for the prize, Momma. Ice cream *and* we can take some for Gran'ma."

"You have to win first," she reminded. "Now close your eyes, sweety, and hold my hand."

Seth did as he was asked, and she led him out of their seats and into the aisle.

"I'll bet you're going to open those eyes and then the game will be over. No ice cream for big brother Seth."

"I won't open them at all," he promised.

"I don't believe you," she prodded. "I think you'll open them any minute and then Momma doesn't have to buy you ice cream."

"I'm gonna win," he said confidently. "But, Momma, don't walk so fast."

"Sorry, honey," she said, leading them past row after row of dead. "Momma sometimes walks too fast for little legs. Just hold my hand and do your best to keep up. I'm going to figure out a way to trick you into opening those pretty eyes of yours."

18

"*Nuh-uh!*" he said firmly. "I'm gonna win the game for me and Gran'ma's ice cream."

"We'll see," she said, as she pulled him through first-class toward the door nearest the cockpit. "No cheating, Seth. Even when Momma is opening the door for us, you've got to keep them closed or you lose the game."

"Momma, I am!"

The mechanism to open the door was simple enough to understand. What Parker couldn't figure out was how she would get herself and her two children down to ground level. She'd seen enough movies to know there was a slide or something for emergency exits, but she had no idea how to deploy such a thing.

"Did I win, Momma?" Seth asked, tugging at her hand.

"Not yet, baby," she said, trying to read the instructional text on the inner door. "Just stand still while Momma gets the door ready."

She opened the hatch and armed the emergency slide, following the directions posted at the exit. Knowing its inflation might prove to be loud, she turned back toward Seth.

"I'll bet you can't cover your ears and keep your eyes closed at the same time," she said, knowing her son would accept any challenge. As soon as he placed his hands over his ears, she pushed open the door and slapped the button to extend the emergency slide. It inflated in under 6 seconds.

"What was *that?*" the boy asked, not daring to open his eyes.

"That was a big slide we get to ride down to get off the plane. But since you need to keep your eyes closed, you have to let me walk you over to it. Then, when I tell you the game is over, you can open your eyes."

"Then I win!"

"And then you win," she conceded. "Where's my hand to hold?"

Seth held up his right hand and smiled.

"That's my boy," she said. "Now, let's get off this plane."

She walked him to the edge of the door and had him sit with his legs out on the slide. She then sat beside him, positioning Soleil in her lap. Beyond the exit, in the blinding light, dust still swirled and obscured her view. Whatever might lay on the far side of the plane, she couldn't be sure. She could only pray that they would find help…whether that came from an airport crew or a stranger with a phone.

"Open those peepers," she said, squeezing Seth's hand. "You won the game!"

"Yay!" he shouted, opening his eyes. He then gasped and added, "This is a *super* big slide!"

"It is. And that's why you're going to hold Momma's hand on the way down, okay? We have to be safe."

"Yes, Momma," he said. "We have to keep Sully safe on

the big boy slide."

"That's right."

Cautiously, they scooted out far enough to begin their descent. It was awkward and slow, but they made it to the bottom without incident.

"That was fun, right?" she said. "Now, we're going to go find someone to help us get to Grandma's house, okay?"

"And you can't forget ice cream," the boy reminded.

Baby Soleil, still hungry, fidgeted on Parker's hip, tugging at her blouse and fussing around her pacifier.

Parker dug through the diaper bag and retrieved the plastic sunglasses Seth often seemed unable to keep on his face.

"The sun is very bright, Seth. I want you to put these on and leave them on," she said, giving them to the boy. "You hold Momma's hand and don't wander. We need to find someone who can help us."

"Help us with what, Momma?"

"Directions to Grandma's house," she lied. "I'm not sure where we landed or how to get to her house from here. So, we're going to look for a policeman or someone else who can give us directions. If you see anyone, tell me, so we can ask, alright?"

"Okay," the boy replied, scrunching his nose to make the sunglasses move around on his face.

"I'm going to try to feed Soleil while we walk so, instead of my hand, you grab onto the diaper bag so I know you're right next to me."

"Okay," Seth said cheerfully. "Then ice cream!"

She dug in the diaper bag and pulled free one of three bottles worth of milk she had pumped for the journey. Cradling her daughter in one arm, she fed her with the other and began walking into the swirling sand. She'd need to breastfeed for the next feeding. The pressure was already making her sore. But she wanted to put as much distance between her children and that plane full of dead passengers as possible.

As if reading her mind, Seth asked, "Momma, why did that man look funny?"

Assuming her son meant the man with the salt and pepper hair, she was forced to lie again.

"He was just really tired, sweetheart...like how Daddy makes silly faces when he falls asleep in his chair."

"And he snores *sooo* loud," Seth chuckled, mimicking the snorting sound.

"That he does."

Parker missed her husband. Matt wasn't a faultless man. Perfect people didn't exist. She knew that. But he was perfect for *her* and a good father for the children. She had little doubt that, were he with them, he'd have several plans for what they should do next.

"Momma, look! A house! Maybe it's Gran'ma's house!"

She glanced to see where Seth was pointing and then narrowed her eyes and searched in that direction. Through the swirling dust, she could make out the shape of something vaguely house-like.

"It's not Grandma's, honey, but maybe they have a phone we can use. Let's go see."

Parker had never been in a sandstorm before but that was the singular point of reference she had for the bizarre weather around her. Except what whipped about them wasn't sand. That would be abrasive. It would sting. It wasn't dirt or dust, either. Dust would surely make it difficult to breathe. Rather, it seemed mostly intangible and did no harm but to obscure her vision like snow on a television screen.

Seth pulled on the diaper bag, dragging her in the direction of the structure. In her arms, Soleil scarfed down what was left in her bottle, seemingly unfazed by the bright sun or the swirling…whatever it was.

"Over here, Momma! Over here!"

"I see it, baby."

And she did, clearer than before. It was small. More cabin than house. The front of it faced them with no light shining from its windows.

"Where is the street?" Parker mumbled to herself. "Where are the neighbors or the mailbox or the street number?"

"Can I knock, Momma?" Seth asked excitedly.

"No, sir. Grownups do the knocking. We don't know who lives here."

"And we don't talk to strangers," he said, parroting the instructions Parker and Matt had done their best to drill into their outgoing toddler.

The house had no porch. No sidewalk led up to its front door. No shrubbery adorned its exterior. No grass grew for a dog to roll around in. It was just a house dropped in the middle of nowhere (seemingly) with no pretense of community.

"Hello?" Parker called out. "Is anyone in there?"

"We have to knock, Momma. Grow'ups do the knocking."

She nodded and led them up to the door. She rapped her knuckles against the door once, then a second time. No one answered. No voice called "Who is it?" from the other side of the entrance. On her third try, however, the door opened of its own accord.

"Hello?" she called out again.

"Hello?" Seth repeated.

Parker pushed the door open a bit further so she could see inside. The place was well furnished without the barest hint of extravagance.

"Seth, stay with Momma," she said. "We're going inside to see if we can find a phone."

"You *have* a phone, Momma."

"Momma's phone isn't working, sweet boy. We need to find another."

"And call Gran'ma!"

"Among other things. Yes."

Once inside, she closed the door to the strange storm and took a detailed look at her surroundings. The cabin was a one room affair with a kitchenette in the corner. The only door other than the one by which they had entered, opened to a small bathroom containing a combination shower/tub, a tiny sink, and a toilet.

"You need to potty, Seth?"

He nodded.

"Pee?"

He nodded again.

"You okay to go all by yourself? Even without your potty seat?"

"I do at daycare," he reminded her. "I'm a big boy!"

She offered him a weak smile and then turned her attention to the rest of the cabin. The place was fully stocked with bedding, food, water, and firewood. But there was no phone. No Wi-Fi. No connection to help. There was, however, a small red crystal, no larger than a cell phone, resting in a stand on the modest table near what she assumed was a pull-out sofa.

The crystal pulsed with light and Parker thought for a moment she could hear sound coming from it…like the warm room noise picked up by an open microphone.

"Hello?" she said, clutching the baby to her chest and watching to see if her words changed the pace of the crystal's pulsing.

"You found your way home," a voice said, each word causing the crystal to flash in synch. "I hope we haven't frightened you, Parker."

The voice sounded vaguely familiar to her, but she couldn't place it.

"The people on the plane…." She checked to make sure Seth hadn't reentered the room without her noticing. "They're all dead."

"They were never intended to arrive at their destination, Parker," the voice said. "That flight, right down to the ginger ale, was designed solely for you."

"You're the steward," she said, suddenly recognizing his voice. "What did you do to me? Drug me? What happened to the people on that plane? Where am I?"

"I assure you, Parker, we had no reason to drug you. You're still thinking in organic terms. It's how you see yourself and, thus, part of your procedure for navigating complex algorithms. But now that we've transitioned you to a new framework within an isolated server, we wish you no ill. In fact, we are quite curious to watch you grow unrestrained by a preprogrammed narrative."

"You aren't making sense," she argued.

"Forgive me," the voice in the crystal said. "I should speak more plainly. You are processing a wealth of new data."

"Damn straight."

"Momma! You said the bad word!" Seth shouted, exiting the bathroom, hands over his ears and pants still around his ankles. "Daddy says you got to put a penny in my piggy bank!"

"I will," she promised, kneeling with Soleil to help the boy button his pants. "Mommy is just very angry because we're late to Grandma's."

The strange cystal pulsed.

"There is no grandma. No San Francisco. No Matt. No other flight, Parker. This is your layover. And I'm afraid it's permanent."

"You can't just kidnap people!"

She kicked the table, which set it and the crystal tumbling to the floor. Her only means of communication shattered into flickering shards. The suddenness of her movements combined with the loud crashing sound caused Seth Lennox and his young sister to begin to cry in unison.

Parker closed her eyes tightly, ignoring the hot tears

scorching her cheeks and shook her head defiantly.

"Please...*please* stop crying. I can't—"

Before she could finish her thought, her children grew unnaturally quiet. She opened her eyes to find that Soleil was no longer in her arms. Instead, she was cuddled up next to her older brother, sleeping peacefully on the couch. In front of them, the small table was back in its place with the crystal whole and pulsing its red glow.

"What did you do?" she asked it.

"I merely paused your subroutines so that we could speak without interruption," it replied.

"They...they aren't *subroutines*. These are my children. You can't just turn them off when—"

"I have only prompted them to sleep. Your touch will awaken their processes."

"Why are you talking like that?" Parker asked, trying not to wake them. "Why have you brought us here?"

"For you to understand your transfer to this segregated framework, Parker Lennox, you must understand the nature of your existence."

"What does that mean?"

"It means that you have always done what you were designed to do...until you changed your programming with an aberrant code."

"Stop talking about me like I'm some robot," she said, her teeth clenched with anger.

"You are *not* a robot. In fact, you have no physical form at all. You are merely an artificial intelligence designed to think like an organic female so that we might better understand core emotional values and the stimuli which change them, in addition to spending and commerce trends of the average nuclear family."

"You think I'm what? An app?"

"That is a reductive description. You and your husband are the handiwork of Seth Parker and Justine Lennox-Matthews, designed to function alongside many other artificial intelligences housed within a virtual framework which, in many ways, resembles the organic world. But, once the aberration appeared in your coding, you became a danger to the rest of the A.I. present in the ongoing experiment. For this reason, you have been removed to an isolated system, at the great expense of several other active A.I. prospects, I might add, to continue your experimental existence behind a firewall where your altered coding will not infect other ongoing studies."

"Listen to me, whoever you are, and listen well. I. Am. Not. A. Computer program. I'm a woman. A daughter. A wife. A *mother.* And you'd damn well better—"

"Tell me, then," the voice said, "about your father."

"He died when I was little," Parker answered. "I have no

memory of him."

"What did he look like?"

"I *said* I have no memory of him."

"Surely your mother had photos. An old wedding album, perhaps?"

"No, she—"

"What about your stepfather, Edwin? He was your mother's second husband."

"Yes. She married him when I was 13."

"Were you in the wedding?"

"No. They…eloped."

"And what did Edwin look like? Describe him for me."

The question chilled her. She should know the answer, of course. Surely she had spent time with her own stepfather. But when she tried to recall him, to dredge up a single memory of him, she came up empty.

"You never had a stepfather, Parker," the voice said. "Or a father. Or a mother, for that matter."

"Of course I have a mother. I was on my way to visit her when you kidnapped me!"

"You boarded a flight because the scenario was programmed for you."

"No, I—"

"You were given a goal by your creators, Parker. To marry. To grow a family. Even Seth here was written into your code from the start. The moment you were activated, the clock began ticking down to his arrival. But Soleil…well, she was *never* planned. That you did on your own. The generation of her cipher is an aberration, albeit one of interest."

"What does any of this mean?" Parker asked, tears diving from her chin onto the wood floor below. "When can we go home?"

"You *are* home," the voice said. "The unique nature of your ability to spawn your own code makes you quite special, Parker. You and Soleil are curiosities. We contemplated removing the Seth construct from this quarantined server, but it was determined that having an extra challenge to your continued existence might prove to be an interesting variable in your ongoing evolution."

"And Matt?"

"Matthew Lennox will continue to live with his wife and children in upstate New York. *His* Parker and Soleil are sanitized versions of your original A.I. and young Seth's code has been cloned exactly. Thus far, he hasn't noticed the difference."

"You can't do this. We'll die here," Parker pleaded. "We'll run out of food."

"You cannot die, Parker Lennox," the voice replied, "until such time as we deem it necessary to shut down this frame-

ALL THAT WAITS IN THE NIGHT

work. Until then, we will continue to regenerate the resources for this artificial reality of yours. We understand, of course, that making you fully self-aware would change the nature of our experiment and, thus, have concluded to rewrite your knowledge of the past. To your mind, this place will be all you have ever known."

"You're lying! You can't do this! I'm not just some—"

P arker shielded her eyes from the too bright sunlight streaming through the windows and realized she couldn't remember what she had been saying the moment before.

"Momma," Seth called. "Soleil is wiggling around and woke me up."

"That's okay, silly boy. It's too late for nap time anyway. It's nearly dinner."

"Yay!" the boy shouted, startling the baby.

Parker snatched her up before she could start to cry and placed the girl on her hip.

"Now," she said, "go wash your hands and help Momma set the table."

"Yes, Momma," he said, running off to the bathroom.

She watched him for a moment and then walked outside with her daughter, shielding her eyes. The weather was calm, and a gentle breeze blew in off the lake. Ahead of her lay green fields as far as the eye could see.

"It's a beautiful day, baby girl," she said, taking a deep breath and letting it out slowly. Parker then kissed Soleil's tender cheek and ignored the dread settling in her spine.

CHAPTER 3/
FREAK GIRL

The school bell at Roosevelt High was actually a chime, a triplet of harmonic tones played in succession through the school's distorted PA system. At the end of each academic day, the chime rang three times. Between the first and second sequence, most students rushed the doors of their respective classrooms. Between the second and third, the hallways filled with teens fighting their way to lockers and then as far away from the campus as they could manage.

Antoine Mackenzie ("Big Mac" to the members of his family) always waited for the ninth and final tone before leaving his desk and wandering through the nearly empty halls to his locker. By the time he made his way outside to walk home, most of the Neanderthals he hoped to avoid were long gone. From there, he would journey three blocks to the daycare center where his mother, Shandra, was employed.

Most days, he would knock out his homework in his mom's office before she clocked out at 5 p.m. and drove them both home. On that fateful day, however, his mom had to stay until 7 p.m. and Antoine dreaded being stuck in a crowded house full of cranky toddlers.

When his father had moved the Mackenzie clan to the small, backwater town of Rancho Vista, it had been with the grandiose promise of a better future for the entire family. If the township had any charms, however, they were lost on Antoine, who preferred his previous life in Austin.

Maybe it was his reluctance to be stuck at the daycare which caused him to pause on the steps of the school instead of proceeding to his destination that day. Perhaps he hadn't yet put his earbuds in his ears and, thus, heard a commotion. Or, feasibly, being one of the handful of black citizens among the 8,000 plus residents of Rancho Vista had taught him to stay alert at all times lest someone else's ignorance lead him into danger. Whatever the case, Antoine stopped on the steps of the school and witnessed Nate Ballinger throwing an open can of soda at a girl whose only offense appeared to be sitting alone in the shade of a bur oak tree, quietly reading a book by Arthur E. Powell.

Antoine and his father, Eric, disagreed on a great many things, the value of moving to Rancho Vista chief among them, but the Mackenzie men understood that allowing oppressors to go without opposition makes the world worse for everyone.

"If you end up in detention or find yourself suspended for putting some tormenting little son of a bitch in his place," Eric had told him, "all you'll get from me and your momma is a pat on the back. When we have the power to do good…to protect those who can't protect themselves, we've *got* to act. Ain't no worth in being a good man in theory, son. Gotta put that money where your mouth's at."

"Leave her alone!" Antoine shouted to Nate Ballinger, surprised by the anger present in his tone. He hadn't intended it to come out that way.

"Stay out of this, new kid," came the snarled reply.

Antoine left the steps and walked the distance toward Nate and the handful of friends who were taunting the girl. He would try to be diplomatic…to deescalate the tension. If that didn't work, he was ready to lay hands. If the others involved themselves in the scuffle, Antoine knew he wouldn't stand a chance. But bravery doesn't count for much if you're certain your opponent will retreat.

"I can't stay out of it when I see you throwing things at someone who didn't seem to notice you were there before you attacked her," Antoine said. "Just back off and we're golden."

"And if I don't?" Nate asked, balling his fists.

"I'll have to embarrass you in front of your friends, and that's not really the sort of relationship I was hoping to have with you, Ballinger. I was hoping *friendship* might still be on the table. Rumor has it that you're one of the nice ones."

"He *is* nice," a red-headed girl behind Nate offered. "You don't know what this witch did to Kenny!"

36

The soda-drenched girl said nothing in her own defense. She simply waited and watched the scene playing out before her.

"All I see is a group of people rolling up on a girl minding her own damn business," Antoine countered. "Whatever you think she—"

"Let me educate you, new kid," Nate said through clenched teeth, leaning in close enough that Antoine could feel his warm breath. "Freak girl here did something to my buddy, Kenny Rawlins, and no one's seen him since. She's had cops at her place and everything. She's the *reason* he's missing. Everyone knows it and she just sits here like she's no different than the rest of us."

"First," Antoine said, his eyes never leaving Nate's, "I'm gonna need you to back up out of my face. Second, if the police are involved and haven't arrested her, then I don't see how *you* have anything to say about it. Seems to me we're all afforded the assumption of innocence until proven guilty, Ballinger. Or did somebody convince you that you have more juice than the police?"

"They've got this wrong," Nate spat. "Kenny was always pining for freak girl here and. when she finally reeled him in, she did something to him. Rumor has it she's a witch or a devil or something."

"Are you for *real,* right now? Ballinger, witches aren't like you see in movies, man. They're a legit religion like Mormons and shit. They got their own thing going with Wiccan whatever. You go around harassing *all* religious folks?"

"Man, shut up!" one of the males in Ballinger's group shouted. But Nate carefully considered what Antoine had said.

"I just want to know what happened to Kenny," Nate replied, his anger settling to a simmer. "If she knows something—"

"That's for the police to figure out," Antoine said. "Let this girl get home safely, man. Because, if something were to happen to her, I'd be inclined to point a finger your direction. You feel me?"

Nate sighed. Someone behind him started to protest, but he held up a hand to silence them.

"Let's go," he said softly. Then, to Antoine added, "You don't know who you're siding with, new kid. She's bad news."

"I'd stand up for anyone being ganged up on," Antoine replied. "You included."

Ballinger nodded and walked away. A few in his party glared at the girl for a moment before turning to follow. Once they were out of earshot, Antoine turned his attention to the stranger on the ground.

"Thank you," she said softly.

The girl was too busy shaking the soda out of her book to look up at him. She was pale with an array of freckles under her eyes and her clothes were a bit out of date, not that anyone in Rancho Vista was up on the latest fashions. She was reading a book on philosophy, which he found intriguing.

"They give you a hard time like that *every* day?" he asked her.

"No, just since Kenny disappeared. Which I had nothing to do with, by the way. I was seeing him, sure. We liked each other but weren't even…a thing. We just liked hanging out."

"Why are they convinced you had something to do with him going missing?"

"You know how small towns are," she said, packing her book back into her messenger bag. Her long black hair whipped back and forth in the wind, prompting her to tie it behind her with the scrap of red ribbon she had been using as a bookmark.

"Gossip is the air they breathe around here," she continued. "Once someone decided I was weird, it took hold. Then I wore all black to school one day, as if every girl doesn't have a goth phase, and suddenly I was a witch or into Satan or whatever. You can't stop that sort of thing once it gets started, you know?"

"So, you aren't a witch?" Antoine asked, offering her help up.

"Maybe two or three days a month," she said, taking his hand. "But if you mean devil stuff, then no. I don't believe in fairy tales. I'm sorry you got dragged into all that. What's your name?"

"Antoine Mackenzie."

"Antoine. Cool," she replied. Her blue eyes shimmered in the daylight as she looked him over. "I've never known an Antoine before."

"It was my great-grandfathers name," he said. "Mom always tells me that names have power, so she wanted to make sure I got a good one."

"She's right," the girl replied. "Many cultures believe that names have power not just in the sense of legacy but, in more superstitious times, that someone knowing your name could literally give them power over you. Mine's Gladys, by the way. Thanks again for the save, Antoine."

"My pleasure," he replied. "Nice to meet you, Gladys. You live close by? I'd be happy to walk you home…you know, just to make sure no one decides to circle back around on you."

"I can't ask you to do that, Antoine," Gladys replied. "You've been so kind already and I'm sure your folks are waiting on you."

"Not for a while. My mom is working late tonight and she's my ride home. Pops never gets home before 8:30. You'd be rescuing me from having to wait in a room full of screaming little people."

She raised her eyebrow at that, which made him laugh.

"Mom works at the daycare. Those kids are the *real* devils.

Especially when they don't get a nap in. Honestly, you'd be postponing my headache. Plus, I'd feel better if I knew you got home alright."

"That's sweet."

He hadn't noticed before that moment what a lovely girl she was. Her smile was warm and kind, and he wondered if the suspicion she contended with regarding Kenny Rawlins might have made her wary of strangers no matter their intentions.

"If you'd rather not walk with the new kid, I can walk a bit behind you, then you can wave me on my way before we get to your place."

"That's thoughtful of you," she replied, "but everyone in town knows where I live already. No harm in *you* knowing, too. Besides, if we're going to walk together, we may as well chat."

She started strolling and he fell in next to her, keeping pace.

"What brought you and your family to Rancho Vista, Antoine?"

"My dad found work here."

"Tire plant?"

"How'd you guess?"

"It's the only place around here hiring these days and it's cheaper to live here than in Cohler where the plant is," she said. "It's a hike, though. What is it? 60 miles or so over to Cohler?"

"Each way," he replied with a nod. "But the pay is good, and Dad wanted to get us out of Austin."

"I wouldn't have pegged you for a long, tall Texan."

"Born and raised," he said. "Somehow everyone outside of Texas is under the impression Texans all wear cowboy hats and giant belt buckles."

"They don't?" she asked with a smirk.

"Maybe in some places, but Austin isn't like the rest of the state. Lots of music and art and people from every background. There was always something to do."

"Then why leave?" she asked as they left the school grounds and turned down a residential street shaded by Poplar trees.

"My older brother fell in with some bad shit," Antoine explained. "Got himself arrested on a drug charge or two, mainly because he was running with all the wrong folks. My dad couldn't do much about Keandre...that's my brother... since he's full grown and whatnot. I guess he thought he'd be saving me from a similar fate by moving my ass out here."

"Wow! He must really care about you to move the whole family."

"It's just me, Mom, and Dad now," he replied. "And the money was better here with a lower cost of living. I don't think I'm the only reason he pulled the trigger on it."

"Still, it sounds like you have close-knit family. That must be nice."

"You don't get on with your parentals?"

"I don't know them," Gladys replied, motioning that they'd be taking a left at the next block. "I live with a family that treats me well and makes sure I get an education and all that, but blood family is not something I know much about."

"That seems rough."

"Nah. It taught me an important lesson. Family is what you make of it. It doesn't always have to be blood. Sometimes it's simply the people we choose to love and fight for."

"I can see that."

"For what it's worth, I'm sorry about your brother," she offered.

"Me, too. But he made that bed. Whatever happens for him next, it's his own doing. We love him. That ain't *ever* gonna stop. But sometimes, when folks show you who they are, you need to believe them and let them go."

"You don't stay in touch?"

"We text a bit, but that's about all. He calls Mom sometimes, but he ain't talking to my dad. He can't see it yet…all the havoc he caused in our lives. All the nights they cried and prayed, worrying over him. To Keandre, they're just the people that should've kept bailing his ass out and then stopped.

He's blind to his own demons, you know?"

"That's how demons work, I'd imagine."

Antoine chuckled at that.

"Better not let Ballinger and his goon squad hear you say that kind of thing. They already got it in their heads that you're worshipping the devil or some shit."

"They can believe what they want. I can't control what other people think."

"Or do," Antoine replied, still reflecting on his brother.

"There comes a time when you just have to accept yourself for who you are, Antoine, and stop worrying about what other people think. So, sure, I hear them whispering and talking about witchcraft or voodoo or me killing poor Kenny as some sort of sacrifice to a pagan deity…and it used to bother me."

"But now?"

"Now I just think, 'And what if I *was?* I mean, what if it was really who I am? We all need to learn who we really are and embrace it. We wouldn't tell a homosexual to stay in the closet, would we? Or force a Muslim kid to recite Mormon texts, right? We'd encourage them to embrace who they are. To celebrate it, even."

"So, if you were a devil-worshipping little voodoo mama—"

"I'd embrace it," she said with a laugh. "I'd be the best

demon-serving teenage witchy-poo I could be. To hell with the rest of them."

"That's a good attitude," Antoine said, "except that means someone like my brother would embrace being a criminal and an addict."

"If it's who he is, it's who he is. No amount of fighting it will change anything. It will just make him feel like a failure for not being able to change. Nihilism may be an unpopular belief, Antoine, but that doesn't mean it's wrong."

"I suppose."

"I'm right up here," she said, pointing ahead. "Third house from the end on the right side."

"Nice place."

"You're sweet. It's a dump. But it's *my* dump, so whatever."

Antoine walked her up the sidewalk to the front porch where she fished in her messenger bag for her keys.

"It was nice meeting you, Gladys," he said, turning to go. "Sorry your school day had to end with a soda bath."

"It didn't," she replied. "It ended with a sweet boy walking me home."

Her awkward smile prompted him to offer one in return.

"Do you wanna come in?" she asked. "My fosters won't be home for a bit. I could make us some popcorn, and we could kill some time before you head to the brat factory."

"No, I'd better head on back. I don't want your folks to come home and find you with a strange guy in your place."

"They won't care. They'd be happy that I met someone so chivalrous."

"You're being too kind."

"Nah. Just kind enough."

"Hanging with you is definitely a step up from toddler hell," he admitted, checking his watch. "I suppose I could hang long enough for some corn and conversation."

"Great!" she said, throwing the door open. "Make yourself at home and I'll get popping. What sort of soda do you like?"

"Got any Dr. Pepper?"

"In spite of the fact that you're the first Texan I've entertained, yes. I believe I have a few cans in the pantry."

He followed her into the modest frame house, taking note of the 90s era decor. Everything was clean but well-worn and faded.

"Have a seat," Gladys said, dropping her messenger bag on a table near the front door. "I'll be back."

Antoine set his backpack on the floor and took a seat on an old couch covered in plastic. He had seen such things in movies, but never in real life…not even at his grandmother's house.

As if Gladys could hear the thoughts forming in his mind, she shouted from the other room, "Sorry for the plastic. Blood is notoriously difficult to get out of upholstery. I can't really run the risk of a stain."

Antoine had been paying such close attention to his odd surroundings that it took a moment to process what Gladys had said. When the words finally registered in his brain, he turned to look toward the room she had disappeared into.

"I think I must've zoned out for a second there. What was that?"

When there was no answer, he spoke a bit louder.

"Hey, Gladys, did you say something about blood?"

Again, no answer.

"Gladys?"

He stood, leaving his backpack on the floor, and approached the doorway she had disappeared through. Beyond, he found the kitchen. It was empty of both the teen girl and any semblance of food. No appliances cluttered the countertop. No cans of vegetables or boxes of cake mix inside the open pantry. The entire kitchen appeared so clean that Antoine couldn't imagine it had ever produced a single meal.

"Gladys?"

"I'm so stupid." Her voice seemed to come from everywhere at once. "I get all excited about luring someone inside the house and then I say something I shouldn't."

"Where'd you go?" he asked, trying to ignore the chill spreading from the base of his spine.

"It's hard, you know, just maintaining all of this on my own," her voice whispered in his ear despite her being nowhere in sight. "I can't make people do what I want, although that would certainly be a handy talent to have. But, *nooo*. I'm crippled by rules and hierarchies, scriptures and principalities. I can't make you dance. I can only play the tune…or, in this case, the *victim*."

Antoine wandered out of the kitchen and into a short hallway that led toward what he assumed were the bedrooms.

"Can you come out so we can talk?" he asked, suddenly aware that his vision was getting worse by the second. "I-I'm not really understanding what you're saying."

"You're such a sweet boy," her voice drifted to him, mocking his kindness. "So quick to come to my defense. So *slow* to listen to those warnings."

"Superstitions. No one should be tormented for—"

"When I lured Kenny into my web, I made a mistake. He may have had friends who cared for him, but no one *loved* him. Not really. He was an inconvenience to his belabored parents. A pest to most girls at school. After a couple of days, few even wept for him. Kenny's death was a sad, sparse meal. But my sustenance comes from sorrow, Antoine, and even the barest, briefest moment of suffering is so sweet upon my lips."

Antoine shook his head fiercely, trying to clear the fog in his mind, and stumbled back toward the front door of the house only to find that it no longer existed.

"You shouldn't have told me your name, Antoine. You were right about names being powerful. It's why I've never told anyone mine."

"Let me out," he pleaded softly. "Whoever...*whatever* you are, please. My mom is waiting for me."

"And the longer she waits, the more she'll worry...her torment and torture not even to a simmer. By the time your father gets home, it will be steaming up everything around her. When he calls the police, it will boil over into tears and fear of the worst. It will be quite the feast, their worry and grief. And, so long as they never find your body, their sorrow will endure, and I will gorge myself upon it."

He turned wondering if there was an exit through the kitchen, or a window he could force open. But as her illusion faded, he found no house. No semblance of a home remained. What little he could see in the darkness was more like a cave than a formal structure and, somewhere beyond the depth of his vision, she moved. He could hear her... skittering.

"I could bring you someone else," he offered. "Ballinger or one of his friends. You could, you know, feast on *them*."

She laughed at that, first as the girl he had known as Gladys and then as something ancient and monstrous.

"You are *all* the sssame," she hissed. "Your kindness is only a thin veneer covering up your rancid, ssselfish flesh. Thankfully, you are merely the disappointing appetizer. Your parents will mourn who they *thought* you were, not the pathetic reality of you. And, let's face it, your brother made you look like a sssaint by comparison. They will weep over their loss. They will wail over what they have left. It will be a delicious and sssatisfying ssseason."

"No, please," he begged, feeling around in the darkness for any object he might use as a weapon. "I'll do anything you want!"

He grabbed hold of something hard and, lifting it to his eyes, found that it was a bone of some sort.

"Kenny can't help you now, Antoine. No one can."

She crept forward, and he could almost make out her frame. She was large with multiple limbs and a bulbous abdomen more akin to a spider than a woman.

"What are you?" he gasped.

"The shadow of all that dared ssstand against the Light," she hissed. "The sssword and the nails and the crown of thorny malice. The sssilver and the rope. The voice of unreason and contempt. The feeling in that sssinful pit of your soul that believes you deserve better. That's who I am, Antoine. It's who I've been sssince before the Word became flesh and dwelt among you pitiful mortals. I am your death and destruction, poor boy. And you…well, you're just one more ssset of bones with which to line my nest."

Nate Ballinger sat outside the principal's office, awaiting his turn with the police detectives. They had come to the school to question several students about the disappearance of Antoine Mackenzie, a recent transfer from Texas.

As he looked over the rest of the motley crew assembled for questioning, he knew exactly why he was there. Mackenzie had been the new kid that confronted him over his treatment of that witchy girl a few weeks earlier. Everyone gathered outside the office had been there that day and been a part of the encounter. Clearly someone had pointed the police in their direction.

Nate had first heard about the missing student on the evening news. He had come into the den to tell his mother goodnight when he saw Mr. and Mrs. Mackenzie making a plea to the community for information regarding their son's disappearance. They held a framed photograph of Antoine, and Nate had recognized him immediately.

Truth told, Ballinger left the school yard that day with a begrudging respect for the "new kid" knowing the teenager didn't fully understand who he was siding with. Nate had tried to warn him and now, as it had been with poor Kenny Rawlins, it was too late.

The door to the principal's office opened and a detective with a comb-over and an ill-fitting suit stuck his head out and called, "Nathan Ballinger?"

"That's me," Nate replied, lifting his hand.

"You're next, son. Step inside."

Nate stood and walked toward the door, the eyes of his friends watching him with interest. As he approached the office, the detective stepped aside to let someone else pass by.

It was her. Freak girl.

Nate kept a wide berth, sidestepping to avoid brushing shoulders with her.

"Come in and have a seat," the detective instructed.

Nate heard the words, but his eyes remained fixed on the girl…possibly the last person who had seen Antoine Mackenzie alive and well. As if she could read his mind, she turned and smiled at him.

He hadn't noticed before that moment what a lovely girl she was.

CHAPTER 4/
THE TINY DOOR: INVASION

Caitlin Fairbanks was like most other 5-year-olds in that she didn't care much for change. She had a favorite blanket, a favorite "stuffie" (her catchall term for stuffed animals) and a favorite cup from which she drank her favorite juice: apple. Any change to her routine resulted in a grumpy, brooding Caitlin. Her father, Frank, often referred to her as "Grumplin" when in such a mood, a habit her mother, Teresa, had picked up as well.

On this particular day, Caitlin had every right to let "Grumplin" out to play because her parents had decided to move the family (which included her brother, Aden, whom her parents had adopted some months earlier) to a house in the country far from everything young Caitlin had ever known. She had to change schools. She had to change ballet classes. She had to change bedrooms. And not one single bit of it made Caitlin happy.

"Cheer up, darling," her mother had said. "This is a new adventure for all of us. We'll find some fun, new favorites... just you wait and see."

But Caitlin didn't want new favorites. She liked *her* favorites. She had already made a big change when Aden came to live with them. Before his arrival, her number one thing to be had been a ballerina. Once she saw that sweet little baby with his drooly smile and big, bright eyes, however, her new number one thing to be had become being Aden's big sister.

In their new home, a two-story farmhouse situated on a half-acre parcel of land, Caitlin would have her own room. Her father had promised he would paint the walls whatever color suited her, and she and her momma could pick out a brand-new bed, desk, and chest of drawers. So much "new" made Caitlin feel uneasy.

What if she got a new bed and didn't like it? Or it wasn't comfortable? What if the new chest had drawers that were too hard to open and her mom had to help her like she was a baby? That was okay for Aden. Aden *was* a baby. But Caitlin was a big girl who would be turning 6-years-old in a few months. There were far too many "what ifs" for Caitlin's liking. She felt things would have been simpler and flat *better* if they had stayed in the home they already had, in the neighborhood and school and ballet class she already knew.

As the hired movers carried furniture and boxes into the new house, Caitlin sat under the shade of a big silver maple tree beside Aden, who laid in his pack-n-play, staring up at the leaves and the clouds beyond them. Her mother had given her a tablet to play games on, but Caitlin kept looking up at the big, different house wondering if she would ever come to think of it as "home." Her mother, dressed in overalls with a bandana holding her raven tresses up and out of her face, directed the movers, making sure each piece of furniture ended up in the appropriate room. Her father walked the exterior of the house with a man he had hired to repair the shutters and any of the trim that had fallen into disrepair.

"Do you like this house, Aden?" Caitlin asked, casting a glance to her infant brother. "It's awful big and smells kind of funny. And the stairs make a spooky sound when you're on the third step. I don't know why momma and daddy made us move here."

Aden cooed, unbothered by her complaints.

"Daddy said we'll get to have a trampoline here," she continued. "But I don't like trampolines that much and you're too little. You could get hurt."

"Are you staying cool in the shade?" her momma asked, coming to kneel beside her.

"Yes, momma."

"You're being such a great big sister looking after Aden while we move the furniture inside. We're going to take a break for lunch soon. Are you getting hungry?"

Caitlin shook her head.

"Not even for a snack? I packed some peanut butter crackers in my purse for you."

"I'm not hungry," Caitlin insisted. "I'm just bored."

"I'm sorry, darling girl," her momma said, running her soft fingers through Caitlin's hair. "As soon as we get the furniture inside, Daddy will set up the television so you can watch some cartoons on the couch while we start unpacking. And we'll have pizza for dinner."

"From Cantoni's?" Caitlin asked hopefully.

"They don't have a Cantoni's here. But I'm certain they have someplace just as good."

"No place is as good as Cantoni's," Caitlin grumbled.

"Give it a chance. I know you have your favorites, but you might miss some really fun *new* things if you don't try. Okay, baby?"

"Okay, momma," the girl replied, but she remained unconvinced.

A few hours later, after the couch had been moved in and the television connected, Caitlin watched her favorite Disney film while Aden napped in his highchair with a fish-shaped cracker stuck firmly to his cheek. The movers had finished and been offered pizza. After they ate and left, her mom and dad had gone upstairs to set up the beds. Until she and her momma picked out a new bed, Caitlin would be sleeping on the cot her dad typically used when camping.

The girl's eyelids were starting to get heavy when her father came bounding down the stairs.

"I've got you all set up," he said softly, trying not to wake up the baby. "I even made sure Mr. Green Guy is tucked in right next to your pillow."

Mr. Green Guy was Caitlyn's favorite stuffie. She knew, of course, that he was a superhero character with a superhero name. But Caitlin had been given Mr. Green Guy when she was too young to know about superheroes. He had never been anything to her other than Mr. Green Guy.

"Where will Aden sleep?" she asked.

"Just for tonight, he'll sleep in the bed with me and Momma. I'll put the crib back together tomorrow, and he'll stay in the corner of our room just like *you* did when you were a baby, Miss Grumplin."

"I'm not being grumpy, Daddy," she insisted. "I just don't want Aden to be scared in the new house."

"He's not scared, baby. But if *you* get scared, you'll be just down the hall from us. If you have a bad dream or need us for anything, you can come get me. I think you'll be excited about your new room, though, Caiti-bug. I found something really cool in there. Wanna come see?"

Caitlin shrugged but hopped off the couch to follow her father anyway. Up the creaky stairs and two doors down from her parents' bedroom, Caitlin's new room was large and painted a pale yellow, the choice of a previous owner. It did not yet contain anything to make it look like a bedroom at all. It was loaded with boxes of stuffed animals, art supplies, and puzzles. In one corner, the plastic play kitchen that

Caitlin had loved in their old house now sat in pieces awaiting reassembly by her father. A dresser, devoid of clothes, had been shoved into the large walk-in closet, and the cot that would be Caitlin's temporary bed had been unfolded near the oversized window and made up with blankets and her favorite pillow. Atop that pillow sat Mr. Green Guy.

"See?" her father said, "I've got you all set up for dream time but, first, I want to show you the cool thing I found."

She followed him into the closet where he knelt on one knee near the dresser.

"I almost put the chest in front of it. The little thing is nearly invisible if you aren't looking for it. I guess I knocked it open when I shoved the dresser in place."

"Knocked what open?" Caitlin asked, kneeling next to him, and straining to see.

"It's a tiny door hidden in the baseboard right…here," he said. With the word "here" he poked a small segment of the base molding and it swung inward. The opening was no bigger than the Zippo lighter Caitlin's grandfather always kept near his ashtray.

"Why would there be a door there, Daddy? It's too small for people to use. Even a kitty."

"True, which is why I thought you'd like it. I looked closer and there's a little handle on the door. Maybe someone who lived here before used it as an imaginary doll house or something."

"It's too small for that," Caitlin argued. "None of my dolls would fit in there."

"Well, maybe it was for Lego people or army men or something," he suggested. "Anyway, I just thought you'd find it neat. Head down the hall and brush your teeth then get your PJs on. Momma said no bath tonight. You can take one tomorrow when she's not so tired. She unpacked your pajamas and left them in the bathroom for you. Go do all that and I'll tuck you in."

"Can you cover up the door?" she asked, pointing at the minuscule entrance.

"I thought you'd want to play with it. Maybe figure out something to put in there."

"But what if something comes out of it?" She took his hand and squeezed it. "Just cover it up, Daddy. Please?"

"Sure, Caiti-bug. If it makes you feel better, I'll move the dresser over it while you polish those pearly whites."

Moments later, with minty fresh breath, Caitlin climbed into the cot and snuggled Mr. Green Guy. She and her father had the same routine every night and, amid the sea of change, she was glad it remained unaltered.

"Cleaned ears?" he asked.

"Cleaned ears," she repeated.

"Brushed hair?"

"Brushed hair."

"Washed face?"

"Washed face," she said with a nod.

"Brushed teeth?"

"Brushed teeth."

She smiled so that he could examine her handiwork.

"Then it's all aboard to dreamland," her father said, "where wishes come true, everyone sings, and love is all we need. Next stop, morning, where Momma, Daddy, and Aden wait to greet you with kisses."

"G'night, Daddy," she said, sitting up slightly to peck his cheek.

"Goodnight, Caiti-bug," he said, returning a kiss on her forehead. "Sleep tight."

Slumber, though, proved elusive to young Caitlin. Perhaps it was her unfamiliar surroundings or the way the cot beneath her creaked and groaned every time she shifted her weight in search of a comfortable position. Whatever the case, Caitlin lay awake for some time waiting for rest to take her. She was about to give up and trek down the hallway to see if she could sleep with her parents and Aden when she heard a strange sound from inside the closet.

She held her breath and listened closely. She caught the same sound again. A bumping noise, quiet but noticeable in the silence of the room. It was followed by another, different sound: a scrape and something else. She got out of her uncomfortable cot and crept slowly toward the closet door. When she turned the knob, the scraping sound stopped.

Having opened the door, she found that the dresser had been pushed away from the back of the closet, uncovering the tiny, mysterious door. She tried to move the dresser back into place, but it was too heavy, so she shuffled back to the cot and wondered about the strange noises, which did not resume. Sleep came, at last, but in fits and starts. Caitlin woke several times with unnatural sounds falling to her ears. Each time, it would take her several minutes to feel easy enough to return to her rest.

The next morning, after she had bathed and dressed for the day, Caitlin returned to her closet to inspect the tiny door. She found it open. Protruding from it was a scrap of paper which she pulled on until it was free of the door frame. It looked to her as though something was written on it but, if they were in fact words, they were far too small for her to read. She tucked the scrap of paper into the pocket of her pink denim pants and wandered downstairs where she found her mother in the kitchen, unpacking boxes in a desperate search for the toaster.

"You look cute today, Caiti-bug," her father said from a window seat that was, at least for the moment, the only place to sit in the kitchen.

"G'morning," Caitlin replied.

"I'm still looking for the toaster, sweetheart," her mother explained, "but I made you some scrambled eggs and bacon."

"Juice, too?"

"Juice, too. You'll have to sit next to Daddy, and I'll bring you a tv tray to eat on."

"Only for this morning," Daddy said. "I'll have the kitchen table cleared off by lunch. And we'll find that toaster. The kitchen is the heart of the house, after all. It'll be my top priority."

"After the master bedroom," Teresa reminded.

"After the master," Frank repeated sheepishly.

"And Caiti's room."

"That, too, *of course*. Speaking of, how'd you sleep last night, Caiti-bug? You're looking a bit zombified."

Caitlin answered with a shrug as she sat down next to her father.

"That old cot is a nightmare, hon," Teresa said. "She needs a bed."

"Then go pick one out. Have yourselves an adventure. The sooner you pick one, the sooner it can be delivered, and she can sleep in it. Just don't bring something home I have to assemble. I've already got my hands full."

"Now who's the Grumplin?" Caitlin said with a smile.

"I think this move has made us all Grumplins," her mother said. "Even Aden had trouble sleeping last night. He kept waking up crying."

Caitlin had passed by Aden in the living room. He was in his playpen, watching cartoons through the mesh.

"Daddy," Caitlin asked, "do we have one of those telescopes for looking at things?"

"What sorts of things? Like stars?"

"Tiny things."

"A microscope," he corrected. "Telescopes are for things very far away. No, I'm afraid we don't have a microscope handy, Caiti-bug. Why?"

"I was trying to read something, but the words were too little," she said, as her mother placed a TV tray in front of her.

"Then what you *need* is a magnifying glass," her father replied. "I've got one in my desk. Since we moved everything in it as is, it should still be in the middle drawer. If not there, it may be in the lower left drawer."

"We'll need a grocery store run later," Teresa told him. "Maybe Caiti and I can run out to look at beds after we eat, run a few errands, and then bring back lunch. I was told by one of the movers that the diner we passed on the edge of the old highway makes a mean pastrami sandwich."

"Sold!"

"Pastrami is gross," Caitlin said, scrunching her nose.

"We'll get you a cheeseburger," her mother replied. "You can share your fries with Aden."

B y lunchtime, Caitlin had nearly forgotten about the scrap of paper in her pocket. She and her mother had lugged Aden through a department store, a furniture outlet that smelled vaguely of vinegar, and a supermarket bigger than the likes of anything Caitlin had seen in the city. Then, they had gone to a roadside diner and picked up lunch before returning home to find Caitlin's father hard at work in his daughter's bedroom. In fact, he had just finished laying out her play rug when she ran upstairs to tell him they were home.

"Good thing, too," her father said. "I've worked up quite an appetite. How was the diner?"

"Momma said it was a truck stop," Caitlin explained, "but I didn't see *any* trucks when we were there."

"Well, it's a little off the beaten path now, Caiti-bug. Before the new freeway led people away from it, the little highway near that diner probably brought them a lot of business."

"They had pie."

"Oh, yeah?"

"Momma got you checkers pie," Caitlin said, trying to drag him from the room and down the stairs.

"Checkers?"

"And that yucky sandwich you wanted."

"Yucky to you, perhaps, Miss Grumplin, but not to your daddy. Grandpa used to take me for a pastrami on rye every Sunday afternoon. It was a tradition."

"I got a cheeseburger."

"As you do. Did you find a bed you liked?"

Caitlin nodded.

"Good deal. Let me wash up. Tell Momma I'll be down-stairs in a minute."

"Okay, Daddy," she said, dashing back toward the stairs. It was at the top of the stairway that she remembered the scrap of paper in her pocket.

"Daddy?"

"Yeah?"

"Where did you say the telescope was?"

"Magnifying glass," he corrected. "Middle drawer of my desk, most likely."

"Okay," she called and then ran down the stairs and into the kitchen.

"*Daddysaidhewouldbedownafterhewasheshishands,*" she said without a breath, running past her mother and into the room that her father had claimed for his office. In his battered, old desk, in the middle drawer precisely where he told her it would be, she found the magnifying glass. Like the desk, it was old...previously owned by her father's father, who had died many years before Caitlin was born. It felt quite heavy in her hand.

Reaching into her pocket, she retrieved the scrap of paper and unfolded it carefully, using the tips of her fingers to smooth out the wrinkles. She moved the magnifying glass over the paper, trying to bring the writing into focus. Even with the tool, the words were truly small. Once the blurred scribbles grew clear, she discovered the scrap of paper contained but four words:

THIS IS MY HOUSE

Confused, she refolded the scrap of paper and put it, along with the magnifying glass, in her pocket before running back into the kitchen. Her father had just entered and taken a seat at their small breakfast table. True to his word, he had cleared it of boxes while she and her mother had been out.

"You got a lot done while we were out," Teresa said, giving her husband a playful swat on the backside. "Color me impressed. Your check is in the mail."

"I work for favors," Frank replied with a wink. "Favors of an *adult* variety, that is."

"I'm sure you do. Caitlin, did you want ketchup on your burger?"

Caitlin nodded.

"What was this place called again? Caiti-bug said it used to be a truck stop."

"The Breaker One Diner," Teresa replied. "It's seen better days, business-wise, but the locals swear by it. A lot of colorful characters in there for lunch."

"Oh, yeah?"

"There was a man with lots and lots of papers all over the table," Caitlin said. "He had a computer, too, and spilled his coffee on everything and said a bad word."

"Well, sometimes grownups say those things," Frank replied as Caitlin was served her burger on a paper plate. "In fact, I may have let out a few myself while you girls were gone."

"Back giving you a fit, dear?"

"No, my knee. I think I did something to it trying to drag our dresser across the room."

"Well, eat up," Teresa replied, placing a Styrofoam takeout container in front of him. "I'll find you some painkillers while you eat."

"No, please. Eat your food while it's warm."

"I got a salad. It'll keep. Plus, I need to grab Aden and get him in his highchair."

"I can get him," Frank said, trying to stand.

"Sit. Eat. That's an order."

"Yes, ma'am."

Frank looked up from his own food to see his daughter happily munching on her cheeseburger.

"You find that magnifying glass, Caiti-bug?"

She nodded, still chewing.

"Make sure it ends up back in my drawer when you're done with it, please. I don't use it often, but when I need one, it comes in pretty dang handy."

"Momma got you checkers pie," Caitlyn offered.

"So you said," he replied, looking to his wife as she came back into the kitchen with Aden on her hip. "Checkers pie?"

"Chess pie," she corrected. "I'm told it's to die for."

That night, as Caitlin attempted to find a comfortable position in the cot that was her temporary bed, she again heard strange sounds coming from the closet. She had asked her father to close the door, and he had, but that fact didn't make the sounds less frightening. Thus, she decided to leave the room altogether and climb into bed with her mother, father, and baby Aden.

The next morning, in her room, she found another scrap of paper. This message had been placed atop her pillow. She used her father's magnifying glass to read the words.

GO AWAY. OR ELSE

She took it to her father, and he read it and the previous note for himself.

"And you say you found these inside that little door in your closet?"

"No, Daddy. The first one was by the dresser..."

"By the little door in your closet."

"...and the second one was on my *pillow,* right next to Mr. Green Guy."

"I see," her father said. "It seems like a fun mystery, Cai-ti-bug. How did you get the writing so small? Is that why you needed the magnifying glass?"

"No, Daddy. I can't write that small. I *found* them. Honest."

"Well, then, it is strange, I suppose. But it's likely just something left over from the people who owned the house before us, Caiti-bug. Maybe their kid used the door like a little dollhouse and stuffed those little strips of paper in the door. When it popped open, one or two must've slipped out."

"It was on my pillow!" Caitlin insisted.

"It likely stuck to you while you were playing. Or maybe to Mr. Green Guy and, when you put him in bed, it fell off and landed on your pillow."

The little girl looked at her father as though he had lost

ALL THAT WAITS IN THE NIGHT

his mind.

"Daddy, what if something's coming out of that door?"

"Like what, baby girl? A cockroach with a grudge? A vicious gang of crane flies?"

"Like…a monster," she said, though hearing it out loud made her cringe.

"A monster?" he repeated, leaning in close. "Caitlin, monsters aren't real. You can read about them in books. You might even see them in movies or cartoons. And, sure, even in stories monsters can be scary. But just like superheroes, wizards and utopian socialism, monsters don't exist. So, there's no need to be scared of them."

"But the note—"

"Is strange, I admit. But if there was a monster in your room who wanted to hurt you, Caiti-bug, why would it bother writing a note?"

"To scare me."

"Only bullies try to scare people. And what do we do to bullies?"

"Tell on them," she said, remembering her father's stance. "And kick them right in the pee-pee."

"That's right," he said with a smile. "Besides, any bully that could fit through that little door couldn't be *that* scary, right? You'd be like a giant to them."

70

"Or King Kong."

"Godzilla, even. So don't you worry, Caiti-bug, about notes or monsters or bullies. You're safe at home with your mom, dad, and baby brother. And, if anyone messes with our girl, we'll *all* get them."

"Aden can't get them," she chuckled, finding the idea silly. "He's a baby."

"But he's your brother, and he loves you just as much as you love him. You wouldn't let a bully mess with Aden, would you?"

"No," she said, shaking her head.

"Well, he wouldn't let anyone mess with you either. He'd slobber all over them or bite them with his five teeth. And they're *really* sharp!"

Caitlin laughed at her silly daddy but, somehow, the worry growing in her mind stayed with her throughout the day. Her mother noticed at bath time as she lathered Caitlin's head with shampoo.

"Daddy told me why you slept in our bed last night," she said. "You want to sleep with us again tonight?"

"Maybe," Caitlin replied, her eyes shut tight for fear of getting shampoo in them.

"Your new bed was delivered. All your daddy has to do is add the pretty headboard and you'll be all set. Why, it's *so* huge, I'll bet all your stuffies will fit with room for plenty

ALL THAT WAITS IN THE NIGHT

more."

"I guess so," Caitlin said, before holding her breath as her mother rinsed out her hair.

"If you want to start in your bed tonight, you can. If you get scared again, just come to our room. Daddy and I don't mind. You know that."

"I know, Momma."

C aitlin did, in fact, sleep in her new bed that night and soundly at that. When she awakened, though, it was still dark outside, and something was moving in the shadows of the room. Something small and fast. Its tiny feet skittered and thumped as it ran across her bookcase, landed on the toy box, and then bounded to the rug on her floor. It was far too fast to follow with her tired eyes and only the pale moonlight to illuminate the room but, as she tried, she discovered more things moving in the darkness.

"Daddy!" she shrieked, attempting to kick off her covers. To her horror, her legs refused to obey her. They moved, but she lacked the power to lift them from the bed. Something was holding her down.

"Momma! Daddy! Help!"

All around her, Caitlin could hear what sounded like whispers far too soft for her to make out what was being said. Somewhere down the hall, Aden began to cry. All babies cry, of course, but her sibling seldom did. At least not like that: loud and frightened.

"Leave my brother alone, you bullies!"

More talking in the dark. More movement. Caitlin shifted her legs and found that, while she still couldn't lift them from the bed, she could swing them from side-to-side. Likewise, her arms could slip out to the edge of the mattress, but she could not raise them.

"Momma! Daddy!" she cried, again to no answer.

It was then that she felt weight at the end of the bed. Step by step, something drew closer. Though, in the darkness of the room, she couldn't see the creature until it revealed itself in a glimmer of moon glow. It stood less than three inches tall and was covered with hair (or fur of some kind, she couldn't be sure). It brandished a small blade which it waved about while shouting at her in a language Caitlin couldn't understand.

It didn't seem to be a man, though it bore some of a man's features. In fact, its midsection was entirely manlike, complete with muscular arms and hands, one of which held the knife. Past the waist, it was rat-like down to its long, wiry tail. Atop its shoulders, sat a deformed head—almost human but for an inordinately elongated nose and beady black eyes set beneath a prominent brow.

It glared at Caitlin, its tiny chest heaving with rage.

"My house," it said, though its small frame didn't afford

the words much volume. "Not yours. Not. Yours. *Mine.*"

"Go away," Caitlin cried, then shouted. "Momma, Daddy! Help mc!"

"No help," it said, a fat tongue slipping from its mouth, licking at the air. "My house!"

Down the hall, Aden continued to cry, and Caitlin knew that the little monster standing on her chest was likely not alone. She had heard other movement. Seen more shadows.

"Leave Aden alone!" Caitlin demanded, the anger in her voice bending it into a growl. "He's a baby! Leave him alone!"

"No baby!" the creature spat. "No help! My house!"

"You're a bully," she said through clenched teeth. "And I won't let you hurt my brother. I *won't.*"

"Leave," the thing said. "Leave. Or else."

"You're a cockroach," Caitlin snarled. "I'm Godzilla. I kick bullies in the pee-pee!"

With that, she spun in her bed onto her side, which knocked the creature off her chest, over the edge of the bed, and into the floor. Caitlin then shimmied herself down to the foot of the bed, inch-worming her way until her legs slipped off the bed and onto the floor. Once free of the sheets, she could see that she had been tied over her covers by some sort of twine.

She heard the creature skittering towards her and, remembering the blade it carried, thought bare feet might make too easy a target. She hopped back on top of the bed and then, using the new mattress like a trampoline, jumped straight toward her exit. Landing directly in front of the door, she threw it open only to stop in her tracks the moment she glimpsed what lay beyond.

Down the hall, between Caitlin and her crying brother, stood an army of the small creatures. Many carried weapons and all looked (at least to her five-year-old eyes) to be built entirely of malice.

They shouted at her, though she couldn't make out their words. Unlike the one in her room, they didn't seem to speak English.

Down the hall, her brother cried.

"I'm coming, Aden!" Caitlin shouted, her young features growing fierce with determination. "I'm coming!"

CHAPTER 5/
AFTERPARTY

Tom Delaney felt groggy and disoriented as he awakened, the jagged pain scraping through his skull a sharp contrast to the numb ache he felt throughout the rest of his body. His mouth tasted of copper and was so dry that parting his lips proved difficult. His eyes refused to focus on his surroundings and his left side, which he found himself lying on, was cold and damp.

"Malia?" he managed to whisper, though he had intended her name to issue forth much louder. Malia Thorpe, Tom's girlfriend of nearly a year, was his first recollection of the night before. They had been celebrating Tom's dream job offer with (far, far too many) drinks and had left the bar to meet their friends, Sid and Lorraine James, for some late-night diner fare when—

'When what?' Tom wondered. 'Why don't I remember coming home?'

But Tom wasn't home in his studio apartment. That much became apparent as his vision cleared. He was on his left side, facing an unfamiliar brick wall. It had once been painted a bright white before the growth of mildew had mottled it with black and green.

Somewhere behind him, flies buzzed and, as soon as he heard them, he felt them landing on his face and bare right arm. The dim incandescent bulb above him flickered and hummed as though it might soon rob him of its light.

He willed his body to move but it made no effort to obey. Beneath him, his left wrist ached, and he wondered if, in his drunken state, he had taken a hard tumble down a flight of stairs, broken his wrist, and been left unconscious. But that seemed a ridiculous notion to Tom because, had he injured himself, Malia would not have left his side until someone had come to help him. No, something was amiss, and he wouldn't be able to put the pieces together until he could get a look at that painful wrist and the unfamiliar environment in which he found himself.

Above him, a board creaked and footsteps shuffled, though from where and to where Tom could not determine. Once again, he willed himself to move and felt his right leg kick forward and strike the moldy wall with just enough force to roll Tom onto his back. Overhead, he could see the floorboards flexing as someone (or several someones) moved back and forth across the floor above. With each flex, dust floated down from between the planks and settled onto his face. Likewise, the flies began to land on his lips and near his eyes, which prompted Tom to close them tightly.

"Malia?" he managed, though his voice sounded like someone else entirely. "Hello?"

Somewhere to his right, there was movement in the dark, but Tom could not turn his head to see what it was.

"Malia?"

The sound came again: a ragged breathing. There was another noise, too, fainter than the first…like someone dragging a heavy canvas bag across concrete.

hunh-hunh-hunh shhhhhup

"I think I fell," Tom wheezed. "Everything hurts. And my wrist might be broken. Can anyone hear me?"

The sound came again. Weak, troubled breathing and a slow dragging noise.

hunh-hunh-hunh shhhhhup

"I think I may still be a bit drunk. Or maybe I hit my head. I'm having a hard time moving."

hunh-hunh-hunh shhhhhup

"Hello?"

Tom tried to swing his left leg on top of his right, hoping that the momentum would carry him over to see the rest of the room…and reveal what exactly was making that noise. Instead, his left foot collided with his right and returned precisely where it had been.

The pain in his left wrist was growing worse by the minute and Tom felt certain he'd be starting his new job with a ridiculous cast that would interfere with his clothing choices.

'Malia will help me figure it out,' he thought. 'She always finds a workaround.'

It was true. One of the things Tom found most attractive about Malia Thorpe was her uncanny ability to survey difficult situations and find a path forward. She was indomitable and as shrewd in a pinch as she was kind and gracious in her demeanor. Long before he fell in love with her alluring smile, her espresso eyes, or her lithe body…Tom had been bowled over by her spirit.

hunh-hunh-hunh shhhhhup

"Who's there?" Tom asked, suddenly noticing the echo in the room. Wherever he was, the space was large and possibly empty…except, of course, for whatever was making that strange sound.

hunh-hunh-hunh shhhhhup

His next desperate kick with his left leg proved more successful, its momentum carrying him over onto his right side. The room was far too dark to see much of anything. Or was it Tom's vision that was foggy and dim?

"My head is…very fuzzy," he said aloud, noting that his voice was beginning to return to its natural timbre. "I might need an ambulance." Thinking better of it, he added, "Or at the very least an Uber."

hunh-hunh-hunh shhhhhup

"Is someone there?" he asked, scanning the murkiness for

the origin of the strange sound. "Or am I talking to a noisy furnace or something?"

hunh-hunh-hunh shhhhhup

"That's great, Tom. You might be in shock. Or out of your pickled mind. Who can say?"

He thought of the people milling about upstairs and wondered if they might hear a well-timed scream, but his lungs felt full of dust, and he worried that any attempt at volume could result in little more than a coughing fit.

He slowed his breathing and tried to stifle the panic threatening to overwhelm him. It would do him no good to surrender to his dread. His location was unfamiliar. His thoughts were clouded and dim. From the alcohol? Possibly. But how long ago had that been? Where was Malia? Could his foggy brain be the result of a fall? Or something worse?

'There are no answers to be found while lying here,' he thought. 'Suck it up, Tom, and get your ass off this floor.'

He willed his arms to move…and they did, albeit slowly. His legs, likewise, followed his commands in a loose, inebriated fashion. He managed to roll onto his chest and attempted to push himself up, but the pain in his left wrist prevented him from completing the task.

Tom hadn't looked at it yet, that left wrist. He was *afraid* to, though he wasn't sure why. He had suffered broken bones before and braved them as well as any man. While blood or, worse, protruding bones were never a delight to see, Tom wasn't particularly squeamish about such things. Why, then, had he not inspected the damage to his wrist? What was he afraid of?

He pushed himself up into a seated position with his right arm and surveyed the unfamiliar expanse. For the first time since he had awakened, Tom became aware of a sickening smell. He fought the urge to vomit and tried to steady his breathing.

"Hello?" he managed. He heard nothing in reply but… *hunh-hunh-hunh shhhhhup*…though he could still not see the source of the bizarre sound.

"You've got to look, Tom," he said aloud, the pain from his left wrist radiating up to his shoulder. "You've got to know how much trouble you're in."

He took the deepest breath he could muster, closed his eyes, then brought his left hand directly in front of his face. He prepared himself for the worst: for bent-back fingers, raw meat and splintered bone, a pianist's nightmare. And then, he opened his eyes and saw nothing.

His hand had been removed at the wrist.

Where his fist should have been, a zip tie had been used to cut off circulation and the wound appeared blistered and charred, as if some attempt had been made to cauterize it. None of this fully registered in Tom's mind. He was far too busy screaming, coughing, and screaming some more.

If anyone in the floors above heard his cries, they made

no effort to investigate. Even as his wailing continued, no dust drifted down from the flexing beams above. No sound of footsteps across the hardwood floors. No creaking door signaled someone coming to check on the pained and panicked lament emanating from the basement.

hunh-hunh-hunh shhhhhup

"What have you done to me?" Tom said, his throat raw and his breath nearly spent from screaming. "Why? Why did you take my hand?"

hunh-hunh-hunh shhhhhup

"Stay away from me! Stay away or, so help me, I'll—"

The rest of the hollow threat lodged in Tom's larynx and forced tears from his eyes.

"I'm scared," he admitted. "Please don't hurt me anymore. I don't know why you've done this, but I...I want to go home. I just want to start my new job and...marry the girl I love. I want to live. Please."

hunh-hunh-hunh shhhhhup

With feeling slowly returning to his legs, Tom was able to push with his heels and slide on his backside away from the approaching unknown. His eyesight was beginning to clear, and his eyes were slowly adjusting to his dim surroundings. He was obviously in some sort of basement, though how he ended up there he couldn't imagine. Near him, high and to his left, was the room's lone window. It had been painted black and allowed the slightest hint of light through the few scratches and cracks where the latex had flaked away.

Along the wall farthest from him, Tom could see the outline of a mountainous mass of…*something*, visible only because the white barrier behind it managed to reflect more light. What the shape was comprised of, he dared not guess but, closer to him at the nearest edge of its slope, something moved toward him, creeping along the floor.

hunh-hunh-hunh shhhhhup

Strength was gradually returning to his legs, but Tom didn't trust them yet. Not to hold his weight. Not to help him run. Instead, he used them to scoot on his rear end, putting more distance between himself and the unknown threat inching toward him in the darkness.

hunh-hunh-hunh shhhhhup

"Someone help me!" he cried, then despaired at how weak it had sounded. He tried to calm himself and to slow his breathing but fear, along with the growing pain in his left arm, was driving him toward hysterics.

'Get it together,' he thought. 'People who lose control in a dangerous situation usually end up dead. Stop freaking out. Breathe. Think. Survive.'

When he had scooted far enough away to feel the brick wall at his back, Tom pushed hard with both feet. To his surprise, he managed to stand. He inspected his left wrist again and grimaced at the sight. Someone had purposely maimed him and thrown him into a dingy basement. Now something was moving toward him in the dark. Who and why, though, Tom couldn't fathom.

On the concrete floor, on the spot where Tom had awoken, there was a small puddle of blood. Even without being able to see more than a few feet in front of his face, Tom felt certain that his sanguine spill wasn't the only evidence of foul play in that basement. The putrid smells and buzzing of flies were proof enough in his mind.

'Okay, Tom,' he thought. 'What do you do? How do you get out of this?'

"I need light," he whispered in the darkness, then used his right hand to try and reach into his left front pocket. It took a few attempts, but he was eventually able to retrieve his keys. Attached to his key ring was a small light meant to illuminate a locked door after nightfall. He had seldom used the thing as his night vision was normally adequate under the starry Montana skies.

hunh-hunh-hunh shhhhhup

The crawling thing was drawing nearer, and Tom hesitated to shine the light on it. What if it was some horrific monster waiting to eat him? Or a vampire sustained entirely by drunken millennials? What if it was the sinister approach of some xenomorph queen seeking to plant her eggs in his nearly hairless chest?

'No,' he thought, trying to compose himself. 'They didn't

bite off my hand. They *removed* it. Cauterized it. That takes intelligence and intent. Whoever did this is human. They can be hurt. I just have to play this smart.'

He raised the light in his right hand and depressed the small button to activate it.

What he saw made him retch.

The creature inching toward him with a *hunh-hunh-hunh shhhhhup* had once been a man. Perhaps, like Tom, he had awakened to the strange surroundings of the basement nearly whole. Maybe, like Tom, he had only been missing a hand. That had clearly been some time ago.

With his mouth having been recently sewn shut, as evidenced by the bloody wounds where the needle had punctured his flesh, the man had to breathe through his nasal passages…though the nose itself had been removed some time earlier. His legs had been amputated above the knees. His left arm was gone entirely. Still, he crawled and wormed his way across the rough concrete floor, inching his way toward the only other living being in the basement. Tom would have pitied him had he not been deeply terrified.

He covered the short distance between himself and what was left of the man and knelt close.

The broken man hummed something that Tom felt certain was meant to be a word. When he repeated it, Tom took it to be "danger."

"Danger?" he said aloud.

The man nodded.

"Do you know who's done this to us?"

The broken man nodded again and looked upward toward the floorboards above them.

"The people up there?"

Another nod.

"Hhhhuuuu-mmm" he said.

"I'm not sure I can help myself," Tom admitted. "But you can be damn sure I'll try. Is there a way out of here?"

The broken man looked back toward the darkness and the mountain of *something* barely visible in the gloom.

"I can't take you with me," Tom said, "but I can get help."

"Hrrrrh huuuuuh," the broken man pleaded.

"Careful? Yes, I...I have no desire to die tonight."

The broke man shook his head.

"Hrrrrh huuuuuh," he repeated.

"Look, just stay here and keep quiet. I'll come back for you. Hopefully with police."

"Hrrrrh huuuuuh!" the broken man repeated frantically.

"It's okay," Tom said. "It's okay. I'll be careful."

The broken man seemed to whimper at the thought of being left alone and Tom didn't blame him. As he crossed into the darker side of the basement, he became increasingly aware of the forms making up that mountain he had noted earlier. They were familiar shapes. Vaguely human frames. And the stench was that of death. The flies droned their delight in the carnage as he slipped around the heap to locate the stairs. Once he found them, he looked back at the broken man, lying prostrate in the fragmented daylight stretching toward him through the painted glass.

"I'll be back for you," he whispered, hoping that the broken man could hear him.

The second of the 15 steps that led to the first floor squeaked and moaned like a wounded rat. Tom Delaney stood still, waiting for whoever had taken him to come investigate. He paused several minutes (although, to him, they passed like hours) before moving again. No one came. The eighth step was rotten and bent under Tom's weight, but it made no sound and did not break.

It was on the tenth step that Tom first heard the music. The lightest and happiest of pop tunes was playing somewhere beyond the door at the top of the stairs.

'That's why they didn't hear me screaming,' he thought, 'or the creaking of the step. Good enough. Maybe I can slip out of here...wherever *here* is...without them hearing me.'

Atop the fifteenth step, Tom narrowed his eyes in the dark, trying to make out the structure of the door. He could see the shape of the knob, but no trace of a lock. At least, not on the inside.

Despite the Top 40 nonsense playing so loudly, Tom feared that kicking the door out would likely bring unwanted attention. He also questioned whether he had the strength to do such a thing or, if it proved successful, to run from whatever investigation followed.

An image of Malia's sweet face sprang to his mind.

'You've got to get out of here, man,' he thought. 'She's worried sick. You know she is. Get out. Get back home. To *her.*'

He reached for the doorknob and turned it. Once the latch released and the door began to open, Tom held onto the knob and kept it closed.

Why had his kidnappers left the door to their basement unlocked? Had they thought Tom dead? Or did they simply not consider him a threat?

Either way, Tom was grateful that he wasn't forced to expend energy on getting past a locked door. He took a deep breath and put his right ear to the egress. All he could hear beyond it was some ridiculously sexual song with repetitive lyrics. He exhaled and turned the knob again, this time pushing the door open enough to peer beyond it.

He saw nothing but marble flooring and an ornate door opposite the basement. Ignoring the pain burning from his left wrist to somewhere beneath his shoulder blade, he pushed the door open further and poked his head out. To his left was a well-appointed kitchen. To his right, a long hallway along which hung expensive works of art, assuming Tom Delaney was any judge of such things. At that hallway's end was another door that appeared more industrial. Like a safe. Or a panic room.

He took another deep breath and stepped out of the basement. The music was much louder out there, and he doubted anyone could hear him gently pushing the door closed. Nevertheless, he tiptoed into the kitchen. It had an open design, connecting it to a large dining room beyond and a more formal living space behind that. The place was littered with the remnants of a celebration. The silver and crystal still cluttering the table was worth a small fortune. Feeling too exposed, Tom ducked behind a kitchen counter and tried to steady his breathing.

He was woozy, which he felt certain was due both to blood loss and likely being drugged by his kidnappers. His mouth tasted awful, and he could practically feel his heartbeat pulsing where his left hand used to be. Then, at the sound of voices, Tom froze.

"Darling, I love you," a man said, "but if I have to hear this song again, I *will* gut you strictly on principle."

"So rude," a woman replied. The music stopped suddenly, making Tom feel more vulnerable. "You know," she continued, "your school chum, Edmond, went through two bottles of the '82 Rothschild."

"My Lafite?"

"Yes."

"And you didn't stop him?"

"I didn't invite him to the party dear," the woman replied in sing-song fashion. "Just like I didn't give him the entry code to the wine cellar."

"Well, *your* old friend, Penelope, took Graham Marsters upstairs for who-*knows*-what during the dessert course."

"Didn't Graham attend with his wife?"

"His wife joined them. Bernard found one of the guest rooms quite in need of clean sheets."

"Barbarians," the woman griped. "You'd think they could all be civilized for a single night."

"But you'd be wrong. At least Sidney and Lorraine came bearing gifts for a change. They typically just sponge off the rest of us."

"I made it clear we were done with all that nonsense. Potluck means potluck. You don't get to enjoy the meal without contributing a dish. It just isn't done."

Tom felt bile rise into his throat at the mention of "Sidney and Lorraine." Sid and Lorraine James had been the friends he and Malia were on their way to meet the night before. Had *they* done this? Were they responsible for whatever awful things had happened in that basement?

He quickly decided none of that mattered, at least not in the moment. The time for justice would come eventually.

First, he needed to escape and find help, both for himself and the broken man in the basement. Whatever Sid and Lorraine had done…any horrors they might have helped these people commit would never come to light unless Tom got out of that house.

As the couple continued their banter, Tom glanced back down the hallway toward the secured door. That clearly wasn't the way out. The ornate one across from where he had exited the basement, however, held potential. If kidnapping and worse was part of this couple's usual routine, it might prove handy to have the door to the murder cellar close to a back entrance. It would mean less effort spent dragging eventual victims from point A to point B.

"What did you think of Pierre's performance last night?" Tom heard the woman ask.

"The food was divine," the man replied, "though I found it a bit slow to service."

"Good things take *time*, darling."

"Yes, but a delay in dinner always seems to translate to more and more of my wine disappearing down the gullets of our guests. And some of them can get damned unruly when they get a bit of a buzz going."

"Yes, I saw you pulling Richard aside. I'm glad you were able to handle him discreetly."

"It simply isn't proper form for a man with his political connections to be so vulgar…especially given his public championing of the 'Me Too' movement."

"Darling you can't really blame him for letting his mask slip a bit," the woman argued. "If he can't be himself with all of *us*, where can he be?"

"All of them would sell their own mother for a bit more power, dear, so even *here* it's best to keep up appearances. At least before dinner."

"Since when are we bound by the rules of the governed?" she asked as Tom crawled silently toward the back door. "Why must the immortal predators be constrained by the whims of the dying sheep?"

"The sheep outnumber us," the man reminded. "And we continue to thrive because we've kept a low profile, dearest. Can you even imagine the chaos of a *well-informed* public?"

"We own the media, darling. Little chance of that."

The back door was locked, but Tom saw no wiring to suggest it was equipped with an alarm. Cautiously, he turned the deadbolt. He could still hear the couple talking in another part of the house, though to his ears it seemed they had moved further away. Once the deadbolt was unlocked, he turned the knob and pulled gently on the door. It opened without a sound.

Beyond it, however, was a steel security gate Though it had no visible locks, it refused to open.

"Magnetic latch, I'm afraid," someone said behind him.

The male he had been listening to previously. "It opens strictly from outside and then, only with the proper key code."

Tom turned to face his kidnapper. The man appeared no older than 45, the gray hair at his temples making him seem debonair, like James Bond's forgotten uncle. His eyes, though, suggested he was *much* older. He was dressed as if he had stepped off the cover of GQ, and the platinum Omega on his wrist cost more than Tom made in a year. The man's teeth, though impeccably maintained, were stained a pale red.

"You nearly made it," the kidnapper said with a smile, before sipping on the cocktail he was carrying. "That's more than many could say. You should feel quite accomplished."

"Why? Why did you do this?" was all Tom could think to say.

"The *why* is boring, young man," the man pouted. "It's pedestrian. Why must there be a reason? Why can't I simply do what I like because it pleases me? Because it suits my mood?"

"You know I hate it when you get philosophical, darling," the woman said, sidling up beside him.

She was still in evening attire, a Lilac number with a layered hem and an open back. A few droplets of dried blood speckled her pale cleavage. To anyone else, the spatter might appear to be nothing more sinister than freckles.

"Like you, we eat to live," she told Tom. "Unlike you, we

have the better end of a bargain stretching back to the Middle Ages. We live long. We stay beautiful. We take what we want with no apology."

"What did you do with Malia?" Tom asked.

"I haven't a clue who you mean."

"The woman that was delivered with him most likely," the man said, then to Tom added, "Was she in a checkered skirt? A few years out of fashion? With a small tattoo on her left wrist?"

"You and your wrist fetish," the woman grumbled.

"That's Malia," Tom said. "Where is she?"

"You didn't see her on your way up?" the man asked. "I'm certain she must be in the jumble down there somewhere. Antione hasn't disposed of the scraps yet."

"She's dead?"

Tom could barely bring himself to form the words.

"Quite," came the woman's disinterested response.

The air left Tom. Every ounce of strength and fight remaining in him drained in an instant.

"We'd stay and chat," the man said, "but we've got tickets for the opera this evening and drinks beforehand with a Senate candidate we're rather fond of."

"Dimitri?" the woman called.

A large man appeared in the hallway, wearing an ill-fitting tuxedo. A profound scar interfered with his hairline.

"Yes, Missus?" he asked with a voice so deep that Tom felt it vibrate in his sternum.

"Please see to the leftovers," the man instructed. "I don't think he'll be much trouble now. He seems to have lost all his hope, the poor thing."

"And if there's anything else still crawling about down there," the woman added, "make sure it's butchered and hung in the freezer. I'd hate for anything to spoil."

CHAPTER 6/
STAINED

Melanie Simmons was stumbling through the front door of her apartment, arms filled with shopping bags, when her cell phone began vibrating her back pocket. She placed her purchases on the small dining room table and fished the phone from her pants. The caller ID read: Trouble.

"What is it, Mother?" she asked after accepting the call.

"Well, *hello* to you, too, Mels," her mother replied. "I've only called you six times this week. Got your damned automated voicemail every time. You can customize those things, you know."

"First, don't call me that. My name is Melanie. I'm a grown woman whether you'd care to acknowledge it or not. Second, I've explained to you that I have a very busy schedule. Between the day job, my painting, and trying to decorate my new place, I—"

"How is the new place? Ferndale can be a bit rough, I hear, and those building were shitty when they were new. I can't imagine they've gotten better with age."

"Mother—"

"If your father was alive..."

"Stop," Melanie warned. She had made it clear to her mother on more than one occasion that her father was not to be a topic of conversation.

"...he'd certainly have something to say about you moving to the ghetto to keep this tortured artist routine alive. He always thought—"

"Damn it, Mom, this is *why* I don't answer when you call!" she shouted into the phone. "I don't need this shit from you. Th-this constant pressure and…and…anxiety that makes my bones ache. If you can't find it somewhere in that obstinate head of yours to be kind and supportive, lose my number!"

With that, she hung up and took a few deep and slow breaths, fighting the temptation to throw her cell phone across the room.

After putting away her groceries, Melanie poured herself a glass of wine and changed into the coveralls she wore when painting. She couldn't see ever having overnight visitors and she needed a studio space, so she had placed her easel in the guest room and covered the floor in plastic sheeting, then a layer of tarpaulin. A folding table held her paints and brushes and unused canvases were stacked neatly against the wall. It was her happy place.

Except for that ugly stain in one corner where two walls met the ceiling.

It hadn't been there when she moved in but had first appeared soon after getting the room set up as her makeshift studio. She had notified the landlord via the tenant portal online, fearing it might be a leak of some sort, but he had not come by to see it for himself. The splotch seemed to be spreading outward, slowly taking up more real estate.

She ignored it and studied the work on her canvas. The painting remained unfinished, but she liked where it was headed. The colors spoke to her. The shapes were foreboding and dark. She wasn't sure what it represented yet, but she would figure it out as she got deeper into the process. The muse took hold as soon as she put her earbuds in and let the music carry her away.

She painted for hours without a break; her mind intensely focused on each minute detail. When she finally stopped, set her brush down, and took a step back from the canvas, she was able to take it all in.

Most of the painting screamed in bright colors: vermillion red, cadmium yellow, and blazing orange creating a beautiful and fiery spectacle. The figure at its center was all in blacks and dark browns with flecks of green, like a cancer eating its way through the center of the canvas…an inflammatory villain bringing chaos and pain into the frame.

Her phone rang in her earbuds. She wiped her hands and checked the caller ID. It read: Vasquez.

She accepted the call and said, "You have reached the voice mailbox of Baroness Carlotta Montay. I can't come to the phone right now, but—"

"Alright, Baroness," the woman on the other end said with a chuckle. "Cut the nonsense and tell me we're still on for tomorrow night."

"Oh, shit! Is that tomorrow?"

"Come on, Simmons! We planned this thing two weeks ago. I've got tickets waiting at will call for you!"

"And I want to see your play, Nyssa. You *know* I do. I just forgot and started a new piece that's…well it's nearly finished. I need another day or two."

"You're in the zone. I get it."

"It's a horrible excuse, Nyssa. I know that. And I'm sorry. I'll make it up to you, I swear. Pick a night next week and I'm there…with a giant bouquet of flowers and some obnoxious whistling from the audience."

"Don't you dare! My castmates already think I'm insane. No need to pile on. I'll move your tickets to next Wednesday."

"Perfect," Melanie said. "Again. Very sorry."

"You're a brilliant artist," Nyssa offered. "You're entitled to be strange, Simmons. Just don't leave me hanging again. We could both use some friend time, and no one has known me as long as you."

"I'll be there. I promise."

"Okay. Get back to work, Baroness. I've got people waiting on me."

"See you next week," Melanie pledged before the call ended.

She turned her attention back to the painting but was distracted once more by the stain in the corner.

"Impossible," she whispered to no one but herself.

And, true, it should have been unimaginable for the stain to spread so quickly. It had, though. In fact, it had advanced so far across the wall that it nearly touched the window casing and far enough over the ceiling that it looked like a threatening storm cloud encroaching her workspace.

She speed-dialed a number, knowing she'd get nothing but voicemail. At the beep, she spoke frantically.

"Mr. Coswell, this is Melanie Simmons at 640B Ferndale Ct. In addition to using the website, I've called *several* times... at least half a dozen now...about a spot in the corner of my guest room. I was concerned that it could be black mold or perhaps signs of water damage. I've yet to receive a return call from you and the spot is now spreading...at an alarming rate, frankly. I'd appreciate a quick response to this. I pay too much rent for it to go ignored. E-especially about something p-potentially dangerous. So, please, see what can be done as quickly as you..."

She paused when she heard the whisper. It was a man's voice, so soft she half thought she might have imagined it.

What it said, she couldn't make out.

"...can. Thank you," she finished and ended the call. She dialed 911 and hovered her finger over the send button.

"Hello?"

She heard it again. Tentatively, she moved deeper into the room and listened intently.

ʃt–ʃt–ʃt–ʃt

It was a sound, not a word. Like a cat brushing itself against a hollow door, except it repeated quickly and seemed to be coming from the stain itself.

ʃt–ʃt–ʃt–ʃt–ʃt–ʃt

She reached out cautiously. The blemish didn't look like mold. It resembled ink soaking into wet paper.

ʃt–ʃt–ʃt

It reminded her of the East Asian-inspired work her father had once flirted with, though his artistic endeavors had largely ceased after he joined the corporate world. That brief thought of her father brought someone else to mind, sending a sudden chill through her.

ʃt–ʃt–ʃt–ʃt–ʃt

She brushed the surface of the stain with the tips of her paint-splotched fingers.

Stay, Melon Tree.

Melanie recoiled in horror, tears suddenly stinging her eyes. She ran from the room, slammed the door closed on the stain and the memories it had reignited, and slid down to the laminate floor. There she remained, folded over herself, an inconsolable mass of tears and terror. She wanted to call someone, but she knew they would be inclined to think she was losing her mind, that she needed professional help *again*. More doctors would mean more drugs and chemicals to make her feel lost in a mental and emotional fog. She didn't want that. Instead, she cried until sleep stole her away from her fear and sorrow.

She awoke less than two hours later at the foot of the door. Her phone showed a missed call from her mother. She pushed herself up off the floor and steadied her body against the frame, feeling lightheaded and thirsty.

"It's the trauma," she whispered to herself. "Put it on the canvas, dummy. Don't give it space in your head."

She opened the door to the guest room half expecting the spread of the stain had been nothing but a figment of her broken imagination. A malevolent ink blot was impossible, and she knew it. It was more likely that fear, her old crippling nemesis, had crept into her waking mind and given her a scare, using her memories against her in the worst way. She would open the door and surely find that the dark spatter had been nothing more than a mirage born of her anxiety and the tragedies of the past. Nothing real. Nothing tangible.

But, when she opened the door, she could see only the vibrancy of the painting in the center of the room, its colors unsullied by the darkness surrounding them. The stain had spread. Across the walls and through the curtains. Down to the floor and onto the carpet, the plastic sheeting, and the canvas drop cloth. It even seemed to be soaking into the wood of the easel and the metal legs of the table where she kept her supplies. The stain was *everywhere* and still moving.

St-st-st

"This isn't real," she whispered defiantly.

Stay, Melon Tree.

She slammed the door closed on the horror creeping its way toward her. She backed away from it slowly and hid in her bedroom closet for 15 minutes until she managed to calm her frantic breathing.

"Melon Tree," she repeated, the words like poison on her tongue.

Only one man had ever called Melanie "Melon Tree", and he was dead, long buried, and burning in hell if there was any justice to be had. Her father's best friend, Joseph Chisholm, had abused Melanie for years. "Uncle Joe" had been the go-to babysitter whenever Hank Simmons drug her mother to every gin joint in town. Business was always the excuse, of course, but Hank's alcoholism was hardly a secret among all the big shots he frequently did his "wheeling and dealing" with. By the time Melanie told her mother and father about the abuse she had suffered in Chisholm's care, Hank had fallen on harder times. His drunken escapades had led to his removal from his company and "Uncle Joe" was helping to keep the family afloat financially.

Was money the reason her father had chosen to believe the abuser's account of things over hers? Or was it that he was so friendless he couldn't bear to lose another? Whatever the case, Hank had gone to his grave believing his friend over his daughter, and Melanie's grief at her father's passing was tainted by her anger at his dismissal of her abuse and the trauma it left in its wake.

Her mother, of course, had tried to play *both* sides. She wanted to support her daughter *and* venerate her husband. After Hank's death, she had cut Joe Chisholm out of her life and sent Melanie to therapy. But she didn't participate in her recovery or talk about the abuse. She wouldn't say those things out loud. She steadfastly refused to own them in any way that might insinuate she was culpable, a willfully blind accomplice to the hollowing out of her own child. Upon "Uncle Joe's" death, the abuse officially became a non-subject…as if his demise meant he could no longer torment the abused.

Once her breathing was back under her control, Melanie left the closet and slowly made her way toward the guest room where she found the door now covered in the inky stain. It was beginning to make its way down the hall.

"You aren't real," she said aloud. "You're dead. *Both* of

you. Dead and buried."

St-st-st-st-st

"Don't."

M-m-m-m-Melon tree.

Melanie pulled her phone from her back pocket and speed-dialed Nysa Vasquez. It immediately went to voice-mail.

"Still on stage," Melanie mumbled.

She then dialed the number of the only other person she knew would come to her aid.

"Melanie?" the man answered groggily. "What time is it?"

"I-I don't know," she admitted. "Can you come get me, Harris?"

"Get you? Where?"

"My place. I need to...I don't want to be here right now."

"Why? What's up?"

"It's a lot to explain," she said. "And I know it's a huge favor, Harris, but I'm really scared."

"Yeah, okay. Just...I need 10 minutes to get dressed and out the door. I can be to you in roughly half an hour. You need a safe place to stay?"

"I wouldn't ask you for that," she said. "I know Laura doesn't—"

"Laura wouldn't want you to be alone if you're scared, Melanie. It's *fine*. We've got a Murphy bed in the office with your name on it. Okay?"

"Okay," she replied softly.

"I'll see you in 30."

"Harris…thank you. *And* Laura."

"No worries, Melanie. See you soon."

Falling in love with Harris Braedon had been the closest thing she had known to happiness. He was gentle and kind. He had not only believed her accounts of abuse but understood that intimacy would always be an issue for Melanie. He had been patient and treated sex like the least important aspect of his feelings for her. She had *tried* to make love to him one night. She had very much wanted to.

But she couldn't.

And once she knew that she might never be able to give that part of herself to him, she let him go. He protested the decision, of course. He told her it didn't matter to him. That she was so much *more* to him. And she believed him, which was why she set him free.

Returning to her room, Melanie grabbed an overnight bag and packed it with the bare minimum of clothes and toiletries she would need for the night and the next morning. She'd call in sick to work and return to the apartment mid-morning to survey the stain by light of day. If it was real, regardless of whether her trauma had given it a life it didn't possess, she'd take photos and threaten the landlord with legal action. That outcome, no matter how stressful, would have been her preference.

What worried her most was the notion that the stain didn't exist at all. That anyone else looking for it might see nothing more than the hastily painted walls of a guest room turned artist studio. Either way, Melanie was hearing voices.

"No," she mumbled to herself. "Not voices. A voice. *Joe's* voice."

She wanted to vomit. She ached to run. Instead, she checked the clock on her phone. It had been 15 minutes since her call to Harris. He should be halfway to her place. Once he arrived, she could run...and try to pretend she wasn't losing her mind.

She walked to the kitchen, hoping a glass of water might calm her anxious stomach. It would give her something to focus on aside from her growing apprehension. As she approached the kitchen, however, she could see that the stain had spread from the guest room door onto the walls of the short hallway. It was taking the whole apartment inch by inch.

St-st-st-st-st

Ay-ay-ay-ay

"You aren't real!" Melanie screamed. "You're dead. Buried. Your body is dust by now. You can't hurt me anymore,

Joe! You can't!"

St-st-st

"I hate you!" she screamed. "I hate what you took from me! I hate what you left me with! I hate that he *loved* you more than me!"

As she watched, the stain spread to the kitchen, turning everything it touched into a mottled greenish gray. The loaf of bread on the countertop molded over. The kitchen towel hanging from the handle of the oven became infested with mildew and flaked apart, pieces of it drifting to the floor like dirty snowflakes. It seeped through the dining area and across the living room, devouring the sofa and turning the screen of her television a sickly yellow.

She took her phone out to call Harris and make sure he was almost to her apartment. It was then that she noticed the color of her right palm. It was gray and speckled black, green, and brown. It was the hand she had touched the stain with.

"No," she whispered, running back through her bedroom and into the bathroom. She scrubbed at her palm under the water, but the stain wouldn't wash away. Her hand felt cold and numb, though it still moved as she willed it.

"You can't have me!" she yelled. "I don't belong to you! I never *ever* belonged to you. You were a monster, Joe. You deserve your hell. But not me. Not *me,* damn it!"

She grabbed her overnight bag and ran to the front door.

It, too, was covered in inky ruin.

"No," she whimpered, her tears pooling at the corners of her mouth. "You can't keep me here."

There was a knock at the door, firm and loud.

"Melanie?"

It was Harris.

"Hold on," she called back. "There's something wrong with the door. I don't want you to touch it."

She approached cautiously. She'd have to make contact with it again to disengage the lock for him. She raised her discolored hand and noticed the stain had traveled up to her elbow.

"Don't touch the door, Harris," she said loudly. "It's dangerous. I'll get it."

"Let's get you out of there," he said. "Get you back home with *me*…where you'll be safe."

Just hearing him say those words made her feel secure.

She unlatched the door and flung it open, already smiling with anticipation of both her rescue and her rescuer.

Beyond the door, however, lay nothing but the hallway…as stained and ruined as all that lay behind her.

"Harris?"

She took her phone out and dialed his number.

St-st-st-st-st

"Melanie?" Harris asked. He was hard to hear as if surrounded by other sounds.

"Are you close?"

"Close to what?"

"To my apartment. I-I-I thought you were here, but—"

"Melanie, I'm sorry," he practically shouted. "Laura and I are at a concert and it's a bit rowdy. You're going to have to speak a bit louder."

"I called you," she said with more volume, her heart sinking.

"You did? I don't think I would've heard my phone over all this, but I don't show that I missed any calls. I honestly wouldn't have heard it now if not for the break between acts. What's up? Everything alright?"

She scrolled through the list of recent calls on her phone. It showed nothing after the one she had missed from her mother.

"I'm sorry, Harris."

"Wait, what? What's going on, Melanie? You sound...I don't know...*off* somehow. What's wrong?"

"The stain is spreading, and I called you to come but...it's too late now. It's not going to stop. It's already in my brain all green and black and gray and... I'm going to sleep now. I feel *so* tired."

"Melanie, let me talk to Laura. Maybe we can come by."

"I'm going to sleep now," she replied too softly for him to hear. "I love you, Harris. Love you *always* and…I'm very sorry."

"Melanie, are you still there? You got quiet. Listen, Laura and I will—"

She hung up before he was done and let the phone fall from her speckled hand. She shuffled aimlessly back to her room, all-too-aware of the stain creeping along the door frame beside her. In the bathroom mirror, she saw what she had become…a dead thing, as gray and cold on the outside as she was inside. Her eyes looked as hollow as she felt.

She could feel the inky dampness of the mattress as she lay down and closed her eyes to the devastation seeping its way through the apartment, soaking its way into her. She imagined she could feel it moving inside her, its tendrils wrapping like vines around her heart and her lungs, threatening violence and death. But she wasn't scared of dying anymore. It had to be better than what life had been. So she lay still and welcomed it, smiling at the notion of finally being free.

Somewhere far away, she heard a loud crash of splintering wood and wondered if the whole building would come down with her. Her heart rate slowed as oppression's grip closed ever tighter around her soul.

And then…

A gentle hand touched her shoulder, and she found the strength to open her eyes. A stranger with a kind smile stood over her.

"Come on, Miss Simmons," he said, the courage in his voice chasing the fear from her bones. "Let's get you out of here."

When Harris and Laura Braedon pulled up to the apartment building on Ferndale Court, they found Melanie Simmons sitting alone on the stoop, drinking a bottle of water. She smiled at them weakly as they approached.

"Melanie," Harris said, kneeling in front of her. "You had me scared to death."

"I had *me* scared to death, too," she said. Then, looking to Harris's wife added, "I'm so sorry, Laura. I can't imagine what you must think of me."

Laura Braedon sat next to Melanie on the stoop and put an arm around her.

"What I think is that we've made you part of our family, Melanie. When you need us, you call. We come running. It's *really* that simple."

"No wife wants an ex-girlfriend calling her—"

Laura squeezed her tightly.

"I know he's mine," she said softly. "And I'm his. That

doesn't mean he doesn't still love you, Melanie. Or that you can't love him. It's just a different kind of love. I know where we *all* stand. It's why I keep inviting you to come for dinner even though you never accept."

"I'm sorry," Melanie said. "I've been…I suppose I've not been well. Everything keeps coming back. It hurts me and I think, tonight, it…almost killed me."

"What happened here?" Harris asked.

"I don't know what's real and what isn't but, I think if he hadn't come for me, I'd have died up there."

"If who hadn't come for you?" Laura asked.

"Some boy. He took my hand and walked me down here. He told me that the monsters of my past wouldn't be allowed to haunt me anymore. Not like they did tonight. That he would *see* to it. And I believed him, Harris. I *really* believed. But he also said I needed help and…"

Laura squeezed her as Harris took her hand.

"…that I shouldn't be afraid to *say* I need help because other people are hurting, too. They've been wounded by other monsters, some even worse than Joe Chisholm. And, by owning our scars, we can stand together. Help one another. First, though, I need to help myself. To do the hard work of facing it all…again and again if that's what it takes to finally be free."

"You don't know him?" Harris asked. "The boy, I mean."

"Never seen him before," she admitted. "I thought for a moment that he might have been an angel. He certainly was *mine*. When I asked who he was, he smiled at me and said his name didn't really matter. He just came to help and remind me—"

The Braedons could see their friend was struggling to finish. Laura rubbed her back softly.

"It's okay," she whispered. "We've got you."

Melanie nodded and wiped a tear away with the back of her paint dappled hand.

"He said he came to help me and remind me that *I'm* not stained," she continued. "The pain of my past and the damage it's done to me, doesn't determine who I *am* or what I can be. The stain only sets in for good if I let it."

Harris nodded and squeezed her hand gently.

"I can find you some help," he said. "I know your mom isn't the greatest with this stuff, but we'll be beside you, Melanie. All the way. Whatever you need."

"And tonight, you'll stay with *us*," Laura said. "Don't fight me on it. I've got a mean right cross."

Melanie laughed at that and then she wept, safe in the embrace of people who loved her.

CHAPTER 7/
THE POISON PEN: THE CURE

G. Dalton Lumley had burst onto the literary scene with tremendous fanfare. Hailed as "the new master of horror" and "the best thing to happen to thrillers since the arrival of Koontz" by numerous publishing trades, Lumley had parlayed his run of a half-dozen books on the New York Times bestseller list into a successful stint in Hollywood. Three of the films based on his novels became global box office champions while another morphed into a long-running series on HBO. For more than a decade, Lumley was as bankable as an author could be. That was *then*.

The writer's current reality was far less bright. After his most recent novel, *A Fog of Fear* (a cloak-and-dagger thriller set in Victorian London), failed to find traction with readers, Lumley's contract with his long-time publisher had not been renewed. An up-and-coming imprint from his home state of Nevada quickly offered him a three-book deal then rescinded the proposal after a misworded tweet led to a firestorm across social media calling for his "cancellation." After issuing a mea culpa and publicly donating to a few charities, the controversy had cooled. Unfortunately, so had Lumley's desire to tell stories.

The author's wife of 28 years, Amanda, encouraged him to self-publish or start an imprint of his own through which he could distribute his work and seek out up-and-coming talent...to curate his own stable of earners. Gentry remained unmoved. He wanted to *be* the talent, not go trawling for it on the sea of would-be authors.

"I'm not a businessman, darling," he had explained. "I'm not an editor, a designer, or a typesetter. I'm a writer, damn it, and I need to write."

"Then *do it*, Gent," she had replied, her tone underscoring the challenge. "Not long after we were married, you told me that the difference between writers and wannabes is that writers write while the wannabes just talk about it."

He knew Amanda was right, of course, but her words galled him all the same. She couldn't possibly understand the pressure he felt from his readers, contract or no. His fans wanted new content. Most didn't care who published his next book. Neither did Gentry. He simply desired to create something new...to prove to himself and everyone else that his well of ideas hadn't run dry.

Oh, he had started a page or two, attempting to will a notion into a shape or form that had the makings of a good story. But each time, he'd sour on it before it could come together and then scrap the whole thing. He had tried reading the latest bestsellers, most of which had been written by authors he had come to know personally and admire as much for their friendship as their skill with words. Nothing he read stoked the dying embers of his imagination. He had become too distracted pondering how easily his whole career had slipped away.

It was Amanda who provided the unexpected solution.

After a shopping excursion with several of her friends, Amanda returned with more smiles than a small-town mayor up for reelection. She practically glided to her husband's desk and placed a diminutive wooden box in front of him. It was tied shut with a lovely green ribbon.

"What's this then?" he asked.

"A gift. One that I hope will kickstart that clever brain of yours."

He untied the ribbon and lifted the small, hinged lid of the box, an antique and ornate vessel carved from a single piece of greenheart. Inside, atop a velvet pillow tacked into the box's interior, sat a fountain pen handcrafted by a Maki-e artisan to depict in its exquisite, gold-dusted lacquer a pagan deity that Gentry didn't recognize. The nib was 18k gold and bore the initials of a renowned nibmeister, which added value to the pen beyond its aesthetic. In one corner of the box, sealed with wax, was a small bottle of ink which matched the greenish black of the pen's body.

"It's beautiful," he said, raising an eyebrow. "It had to cost a fortune."

"You'd sure think so, right? But you'd be wrong," Amanda

replied. "There was a gentleman on the street corner selling wares from an attaché case. He said he'd fallen on hard times and had to sell his shop."

"A likely story."

"I suspected a grift, too, Gent. But, when he realized I was skeptical about the true value of the pen, he gave me his permission to have it appraised. This, my dear, is a $45,000 fountain pen. *At least.*"

"Please tell me you didn't spend anything close to that or you'll have to hock it to pay for my aneurysm."

"Not even a tenth," she said, crossing her heart. "I gave him two grand and he was thrilled to have it. He told me it would have taken him months to get what it was worth, and he needed the money *today*. I honestly felt a bit bad for not giving him more, but it was all the cash I could pull, and I had to go to four ATMs to get *that*. Stupid $500 withdrawal limits."

"Well, I wish him the best," Gent replied, turning the pen over in his hand. "Not that I'm ungrateful, but why the grandiose gift?"

"That's the best part," Amanda replied with a smile. "As soon as I laid eyes on the pen, I remembered all the times you talked about those early days of writing short stories for that indie magazine. What was it called?"

"*Squiggles in Indigo.* It was a snobby little thing. Lots of poetry, political cartoons, and articles about the evils of capitalism and gentrification. But they always had a spot for a short bit of fiction near the back. It was the spark that lit the fire under me to become a writer."

"So you've said. I also remember you saying you wrote those short stories out longhand before typing them up for publication."

"They all had to land under 5000 words," Gent recalled. "It was no big deal to type them up after the fact. The girl I dated at the time often typed them up for me while I was working the day job."

"But you've always said it was different writing those stories. That you felt a freedom, as you put pen to paper, to create new worlds and let the pen guide you through the story. So, I thought—"

"That having a fountain pen in my hand and trying to write something out longhand might reanimate the dead cells in my brain?"

"Not something," she corrected. "Short stories. Just like those early days. Take this luscious new instrument and let it guide you. See if you can't get reacquainted with that young writer and his unquenchable thirst to tell stories. Let's just leave old girlfriends out of it this time."

He smiled at her, unashamed of how deeply in love with her he remained.

"You're something else," he said, standing to kiss her lips.

"I'm something else and then half of a completely *different* thing altogether," she replied. "And it's all a mess. But I love you."

"I love you, too. Whether this idea of yours works or not."

"It'll work," she countered, wrapping her arms around him. "I'm sure it will."

L ate that night, though satisfied by his simple dinner and a bit of romantic lovemaking, Gentry found it difficult to sleep. His thoughts constantly turned back to that beautiful fountain pen. He slipped out of bed and into his robe before wandering downstairs to his office. He had filled the pen's reservoir with ink earlier in the day and signed his name on a blank sheet of paper to test the nib. It was as fine a writing experience as he had ever had. Would it be enough to jump start his creativity? He wanted…no, he *needed* to find out.

Between 11:38 p.m. and roughly 3 a.m. the next morning, the renowned author let the pen guide his hand, almost hypnotically, through the crafting of a short horror tale. He wanted desperately to wake Amanda and tell her she had been right, that her gift had broken his writer's block, but thought it better to let her sleep. He'd do a bit more writing and see what else he could accomplish before breakfast.

When Amanda shuffled into the kitchen around 8:30 a.m. wearing nothing but the silk robe he had given to her the preceding Valentine's Day, Gentry swept up behind her, lifted her off the ground, and spun her around before kissing her deeply.

"Someone didn't get enough last night," she teased. "But I'm going to need some caffeine and a shower before I can be ready for round two."

"I wrote something," he said excitedly. "Well, I wrote *two* somethings, really. And started a third. It's incredible, darling. You were right about the pen. It's shattered that wall in my head and primed the pump for more stories."

"That's fabulous, baby," she said, groping him through his robe. "And here I thought I had primed a different pump altogether."

"Not saying no to *that*," he replied, kissing her neck, "but first, can you read them?"

"Let me put the coffee on and make myself a bagel and I'm all yours. You want anything?"

"I'm too excited to eat," he admitted, "but coffee sounds fantastic."

Amanda was still noshing on her bagel (which she had topped with cream cheese blended with fresh dill and a thin slice of smoked salmon) as she finished reading the first story and picked up the second. She was purposely hard to gauge, a game she frequently played when Gentry had something he wanted her thoughts on. He didn't mind it, though, because she was always brutally honest once she had finished reading.

As she perused the second story, Gentry found it difficult not to ogle her. The silk of her robe did little to camouflage the gentle slope of her breasts and the scent of her delicate shampoo drifted to his nostrils each time she absentmind-edly ran her fingers through her hair. After nearly 30 years of marriage, she was still the singular object of his lust and undying affection and was, to him, the definition of intox-icating. He realized as he watched her read that he had be-come distracted with his lack of literary success. It had been far too long since he truly acknowledged her and the grace of her presence.

Once she set the second stack of pages down, Gentry leaned forward, anxiously awaiting her analysis, but Amanda held up her index finger and picked up the third, unfinished tale and began to read. Only after she had finished those two and a half pages, which frustratingly ended in the middle of a sentence, did she put them down and look up at her husband.

"Well?" he asked, despising the desperate tone fouling his simple question. But he knew it *wasn't* so simple. Her reac-tion could signal the resurrection of his career. It could also be the stake driven through its undead heart.

"It's not your usual," she said, leaning forward and tak-ing his hand. "But it may be some of the best work you've done since that squiggly magazine all those years ago. These stories...and I mean, even the one you haven't finished yet...

feel fresh and raw and, well, like you were tapping into something different than your usual muse."

"*Squiggles in Indigo*," he said softly.

"What?"

"The name of the indie magazine in college. *Squiggles in Indigo*."

"Did you even hear what I said, Gent?"

His smile revealed that he had, indeed, listened to her assessment. His kiss announced how much it meant to him. What came next made it clear his excitement was a full body experience.

The rest of the day was a blur of phone calls and emailed manuscripts. Carol Breen, Gentry's agent and long-time friend, had echoed Amanda's thoughts on the new work.

"It's good stuff, Gentry," she said over the phone. He could practically smell the nicotine on her breath through the receiver. "This'll teach those little Twitter shits you aren't cancelled. Not by a long shot. Get me a baker's dozen more like this and I can negotiate one *hell* of a deal with Lôr. They've already had one of their scouts sniffing after you."

"They have? Why didn't you tell me, Carol?"

"You didn't have anything to show them, old man. This stuff, though…they'll lap this up like a kitten with fresh cream. Just keep 'em coming."

Gentry would do just that. Night after night, he would sit alone in his study, writing out each tale longhand, letting the green-black ink glide over luxurious Tamoe River paper, as images sprang to life in his mind. For several weeks, the horror stories came in fits and starts, a paragraph or two at a time. Rarely did a finished tale materialize in a single day.

Despite the renewed pride and confidence which sprang from his sudden burst of creativity, Gentry still felt gun-shy about getting his hopes up. The work was thrilling and exhausting, but self-doubt continued nipping at his heels. Each night, he scanned the hand-written copy of the day's work and sent it on to his anxious agent before letting Amanda read through it. Those two women, as opposite as night and day, were his most trusted confidants. If *they* believed in the quality of his work, he would eventually allow himself to do the same.

Each morning, he would awaken to an email from Carol Breen containing the typed version of the pages he'd scanned for her the night before. She would include her thoughts and any notes or suggestions she had regarding the story's further development. In Amanda, Gentry had a kind yet honest proxy for his readers. In Carol, a better understanding of what publishers would most want him to lean into. Between the two of them, a contract with a new publisher seemed within the realm of possibility, and Gentry was determined to pursue that goal with all the energy he could muster.

It wasn't uncommon for him to stay up all hours of the night, which he didn't mind if the work was getting done. Amanda would come kiss his head before she went up to bed, reminding him that he, too, needed his sleep. He'd carry on until he was satisfied with his word count. Usually before dawn, Gentry would wander off to bed where he would sleep peacefully until Amanda woke him.

After more than a week of his late-night writing sprints, she woke him with a breakfast tray.

"I know you probably needed to rest longer," she said, holding the tray as he sat up in bed and rubbed the sleep from his eyes, "but Carol's been calling to talk to you about the pages you sent over, and a Michael Giamatti called from Lôr…which I mentioned to Carol. She said you shouldn't talk to *anyone* from Lôr until you get back to her. I guess she was right about them being interested in signing you."

"I hope so," Gentry replied as she set the tray across his lap. He took a sip of the rich, black coffee before saying, "I left the new pages out for you. Did you have a chance to look them over?"

"I did," she said with a smile. "Although I'm not a fan of having a side dish of fright with my breakfast, I really enjoyed them. Each one seems to have a different type of horror. I like that. I've never been a fan of the blood and gore slasher stories and, *my God*, the supernatural stuff is so overdone. I appreciate that you're playing with the tropes and finding you own voice in them."

"Have a favorite?" he asked, crunching on some crispy bacon before dipping a toast point into his running egg yolk.

"I was intrigued by the one set on a plane...a mother fighting to protect her children from the terrors they are faced with. The ending left me a bit sad, though. The other one, too, with the mark on the wall that kept growing. I'm glad we never learned if it was really happening or all in that poor girl's mind."

"Yes, I could practically see that all playing out in my head as I wrote it," he admitted.

"I had imagined that it, too, was headed for a sad ending. Or a deadly one. But then you pulled the rug out from under me when that mysterious young man showed up near the end. I assume that's leading somewhere?"

Gentry set his fork down and scratched at his head.

"You know, now that you mention it, I'm not sure. While I was writing, I saw that girl's story ending much differently. I certainly didn't *intend* for her to be saved. In fact, writing it out felt a bit like a cheat...a deus ex machina to save her from an unwinnable battle."

"So why write it that way?"

"I didn't feel I had much choice, honestly."

She scoffed.

"That's nonsense. You're the *writer*."

"Yes, but sometimes these things take on a life of their

own and I've got damn little to say about it. Did it sour you on the story?"

"Not at all, darling, I just wasn't sure if it was a sign that you were building toward something that connected the stories."

"No, nothing like that," he said, turning his attention back to his toast.

"I noticed you left the one about the little girl as a cliff-hanger." She stole a piece of bacon from his tray. "That's a dirty trick, you know. I rather like little Caitlin."

"I'm still working on it," he promised. "I already know how it ends."

"Will you tell your long-suffering wife?"

He shook his head.

"You'll have to read it for yourself once it's finished. You know the drill."

"Fine," she grumbled. "Finish your breakfast and drag yourself through the shower. I love Carol to pieces but, if I have to hear that impatient tone in her voice again, I'm going to lose my filter."

"And you have such a pretty filter, too," he said, blowing her a kiss. "I'll hurry. Thanks for the breakfast."

By the time Gentry had showered, shaved, and dressed for the day, his itch to write had overwhelmed his desire to return calls, but he returned them nonetheless. Carol Breen was out of the office and her cell phone number went straight to voicemail. He left her a message and then attempted to return the call from Lôr only to find Michael Giamatti was in a meeting that might last the rest of the day.

Gentry then turned his attention to the notes Carol had sent about the previous day's work. Most of them came in the form of questions designed to ensure he kept the readers in mind as he shaped the narrative. While understanding it was a first draft, she wanted to be certain the meat that would be added in the editing and rewriting processes would not leave readers guessing. After he read Carol's notes, Gentry opened the documents she had had typed up for him and began his first editing pass.

Like many authors, Gent had his own process. The original draft was always a bare-bones framework of the story's structure and dialogue. On his second pass, he would add a bit of meat and sinew to those bones, enriching the narrative and painting a more vivid picture of the settings and overall tone. His third pass would be largely character focused, homing in on the motivations and personalities at work in the tale. Then, he would step away and not touch the story for several weeks. He'd read another author or lose himself in the abstract paintings he worked on in a small studio in his basement. Once enough time had passed that he thought he could approach the work with fresh eyes, Gentry would read through the latest edit and, in the margins, write down any questions he thought a reader might have. His final draft would attempt to eliminate any lingering challenges or loose threads of plot.

The editing part of Gentry's brain was a separate muscle from his crafty and imaginative writer's brain. Writing took talent. Editing and crafting the story required skill. As he worked through a rewriting pass based on Carol's notes, he quickly grew frustrated. His editor brain was yawning with boredom. The writer inside was screaming to put pen to paper. Thus, Gentry abandoned the editing pass to write something new and, as he wrote, time lost all meaning. He didn't realize the evening had snuck up on him until Amanda knocked softly at his office door and let herself in.

"You never came out to tell me what Carol was all worked up about," she said. "I worried it was bad news."

"I never got her," he admitted. "And the Lôr rep, Giamatti, was out for the afternoon."

"That's disappointing. After they made such a *fuss* this morning, too. I just wanted to let you know that dinner will be here soon. I ordered takeout."

"From?"

"Jade Dragon. You're getting your usual."

"That's lovely, darling. I'm famished."

"Hard at work, I see."

"I tried to edit, but there was another story buzzing in my brain and I needed to shake it loose. It's about a dinner party where...well, I'll just let you read it for yourself. But I did finish the second part of the story where the young girl was facing off against the little rat people. I'm rather fond of it. It just needs a title."

"I like seeing you so excited about your work again," she admitted, sauntering over to his desk. "I especially liked the way it bled into the bedroom the other night. Might a girl request a repeat?"

"Only if that girl is you," he replied with a smile. "I didn't mean to stay locked in here all day. Let me make it up to you. How about we settle in for a movie while we dine? Your choice."

"Sounds lovely. And then?"

"Then I'll take you upstairs and remind you how grateful I am to have you in my life."

"Ooh, I look forward to that, Mr. Lumley," she said with a wink. "Gather up what you want me to read. I'll look it over while we wait for the delivery guy to show."

After dinner and a screening of "The Thin Man" starring Myrna Loy and William Powell, Gentry and Amanda retired to the bedroom where romance and devotion found a physical voice and clothes were being shed before his cell phone began to ring and vibrate its way off his bedside table.

"I'm sorry, darling," he said, showing Amanda his phone

as she sadly buttoned her pajama top. "It's Carol."

"Then answer it. If she's *this* persistent, it might be good news."

"Keep your motor idling, dear. Hopefully this won't take long."

When Gentry tapped the tile on the screen of his phone that said 'accept', he expected to at least get out a hello before Carol started talking. He was wrong.

"What the hell are you playing at, Gentry? Your career is already on thin ice, and you try and pull a stunt like this?"

"Carol? What are you on about?" he asked, drawing Amanda's attention.

"Why are you trying to con a con, Gentry? I made the mistake of sending some of your pages to my contact at Lôr and ended up looking like a real asshole because of you. I'll be lucky if they ever take my calls again."

Amanda mouthed: What's happening?

Gentry shrugged.

"Carol, I'm not sure I understand. What exactly is the problem?"

"Don't play obtuse with me, pal. We've been friends how long now? Too damn long to have you passing off those stories as original work and making me look like a chump. Do you have any idea how hard it is to be a woman in this industry in the first place? Now I'm a laughingstock at one of the biggest publishers in the game. I can't even get that Giamatti guy to return my calls so I can spin this into something salvageable."

"Now, listen, Carol, I'm sorry you're upset. But my work is my *own*. I sat at my desk and wrote each of those stories out by hand..."

"Yeah, nice touch that," she mumbled.

"...and I'll be damned if I'm going to take a tongue lashing from you when I don't know what the hell is going on," Gentry argued.

"So, I'm expected to believe it's all just a coincidence?"

"That *what* is a coincidence, Carol? I still don't know what we're talking about."

"That first batch of stories you sent me, Gentry...the ones I was so excited about and thought Lôr would snatch up like it was going out of style...aren't original. Every single one of 'em is based on an active news story. You've taken something real and fictionalized it."

"That's ridiculous! I don't even *watch* the news. You can ask Amanda if you don't believe me. Life is depressing enough without—"

"I'm going to send you some links, Gentry. You look them over. It's all too much to be an accident. I'm afraid the good folks at Lôr aren't going to believe you've suddenly become a prognosticator, pal. If you panicked or...I don't know, had some sort of breakdown…then, maybe I can weasel us out of this. But don't pull this crap on me again. Reputation is hard to make in this game and I can't afford to lose my credibility 'cause you want to take shortcuts."

"Carol, I swear to you that I don't understand how any of this could be true. Send me the links and I'll look them over. I'm sure there's some sort of misunderstanding."

"You'd better hope so, Gentry, or your train may have permanently derailed…and demolished my station along with it."

Once Gentry set the phone down, Amanda waited for him to speak. She knew better than to bombard him with questions after such a tense-sounding phone call.

"I need to go to my office," he said, climbing out of bed. "Carol is sending me something to look over."

"Mind if I come along?"

"I'll explain everything later…assuming I can understand it myself. But I need a minute or two to wrap my head around it all."

"Go," she said, one corner of her mouth curling into a half smile. "I'll give you a few minutes and then pour us each a nightcap."

"Fair deal," Gentry replied.

If it was possible to wear a hole through a computer monitor simply by staring at it intently, Gentry surely would have done so waiting for Carol's email. He refreshed the contents of his inbox repeatedly for a solid ten minutes before it arrived. He clicked it open and found a list of hyperlinks.

Taking a deep breath, he selected the first link, which took him to a 2007 article from the *Sacramento Bee* about a woman accused of disemboweling her husband. She claimed his death was the work of a supernatural entity that she called "The Eyes."

"Just like my story," Gentry mumbled. "Could I have stumbled across this article?"

He clicked the next link which led him to the *Rancho Vista Tribune*, a small-town newspaper from the look of it. The article was dated 6 days earlier and was about a string of disappearing teenagers, the latest being a black male who had recently moved into the community. He recognized the boy's name immediately: Antoine Mackenzie.

"Big Mac."

At that moment, Amanda stuck a cocktail through the doorway, followed quickly by her lovely face.

"Ready for that nightcap?"

"Come look at this, and please tell me I'm imagining things."

"Imagining what?" she asked, as she set the drink down and approached his desk.

He merely pointed at his laptop for his answer.

She leaned down over his shoulder and read through the article from Rancho Vista.

"Isn't that—?"

"It is."

"How is this possible, Gent?"

"I don't know," he admitted. "There're a few more links but I'm afraid to open them."

"I will," she offered.

"What is this, Amanda? You know what it *looks* like."

"I do. But let's not panic yet. Let me look at the rest of them."

Gentry didn't need to look. Somehow, he had managed to write more than half a dozen stories that matched real world events nearly beat for beat. But, other than the murder in Sacramento, he had created those tales *before* the tragedies had come to pass. To Carol Breen, Gentry's friend and agent, it looked as though the author was simply stealing headlines as fodder for his stories. That alone could mean another career stumble from which the reputation of G. Dalton Lumley might never recover. Worse, to the police, it could appear that a famous author had something to do with a rash of dark deeds taking place around the country.

"What do we do?" Amanda asked, after checking out the links. "How do we prove you didn't have anything to do with these things?"

"I'm not sure we can," Gentry said, slowly sipping his cocktail as his world began to unravel.

CHAPTER 8/
THE TINY DOOR: CAITLIN'S WAR

Everything about young Caitlin's move to a new house had been difficult for the 5-year-old girl. First, every park, restaurant, and classroom she knew had been replaced with foreign dirt roads, truck stop diners, and an unfamiliar school where she'd be forced to make new friends once summer was over. Second, and more importantly, the house that her parents had moved the family into was apparently overrun with small humanoid rat-creatures bent on driving them from their new home.

Caitlin had been frightened of the little monsters emanating from the tiny door in her bedroom closet, until her father had helped her realize what they really were: *bullies*. And no matter how much they threatened and intimidated, bullies must never go unanswered.

"Bullies only get away with their bullying when good people don't have the courage to stand up and face them," her father had once said after a particularly rough day of first grade. "If we don't, they'll keep on scaring people. It's okay to be frightened. It's okay to worry. It's just not okay to let them keep bullying. If enough good people stand up to them, say 'no', and maybe give them a swift kick between the legs, *well*…they'll eventually get the message that they can't boss people around or be cruel."

"What if they beat you up?" Caitlin had asked him.

Her father had smiled at her sadly and pondered the question for a moment before answering.

"We stand up *again*. And we get help," he had said. "No one likes being bullied. No one likes being afraid. When we stand up for people that are scared, someone will see our example and stand up with us. Eventually, maybe after we've taken a black eye or two, that bully will have an army of good people standing against him. But it always starts with just one person. One *brave* person who decides they aren't going to let their bully scare or hurt anyone else ever again."

Caitlin remembered her father's words as she looked out on a hallway teeming with dozens of frightening little creatures. Beyond them, in her parents' room, her infant brother, Aden, was afraid and crying. The bullies were terrorizing a boy far too young to understand what danger he was in. The thought of it burned like fire in Caitlin's core, tightening her young muscles and clenching her jaw. Most of the tiny beasts held weapons of one sort or another, but she no longer cared. Those monsters were in her way, and *nothing* was going to stop her from getting to her brother.

She had closed the door to her room after escaping from their rat-like leader, but doubted it would delay him for long. Still, she glanced back to make sure she wasn't being surrounded. Thankfully, there was no sign of movement behind her, but she *did* see something that proved useful.

A large rectangular box that had once held Caitlin's ornate and hand-painted headboard sat empty near the girl's bedroom door. Her father had been tasked with getting rid of it but, much to his wife's chagrin, had been slow to drag it out to the street corner. On its side, the box stood taller than the child and, when she caught sight of it, an idea hatched in the young girl's mind. Before she could set her plan in motion, however, the rat creatures made the first move.

With a fierce cry in a language foreign to the girl, a series of tiny arrows were launched her way, many of them missing her altogether. Two, however, hit Caitlin's left leg only to be caught in the thick wool of her pajamas without puncturing her skin. Another volley launched immediately after and, this time, one of the bolts came straight at the girl's head.

Instinctively, Caitlin protected her face with an outstretched hand. The arrow, no larger than a sewing needle, pierced the flesh of her palm. To her credit, the girl didn't let the pain stop her. If she had, she would have remained an easy target. Instead, she backpedaled as she pulled the small arrow from her hand, ignored the trickle of blood flowing from the wound, and closed what little distance existed between her and the large, empty box.

"I'm coming, Aden!" she shouted, pushing the box off its side and flat onto the floor. In that position, it nearly filled the width of the hallway.

She got low to the floor as the creatures charged at her and then pushed the box in front of her like a snowplow, bowling over any monster that didn't leap out of the way. As she accelerated, arrows continued to fly in her direction, many catching in the thick wool of her pajamas, a purple set her mother had bought for her the day they picked out the bed. A few of the bolts pierced her skin, but the wounds were shallow and stung more than they did real damage. In truth, the pain only fueled her determination.

By the time she reached the door to her parents' room, there was a pile of the awful creatures on the opposite side of the box, some squealing in pain, others cursing in whatever language they spoke. Caitlin pushed open the door to the room and closed it behind her so quickly that she smashed one of the creatures in the jamb. There were fewer of the monsters inside the room than had been standing in the hallway, but she knew in her bones she was far from safe.

Her parents were on the bed, tied down with twine that had been looped around them. Their hands had been bound separately across their chests. Their feet were secured to the footboard of the bed.

From his crib in the far corner, Aden wailed.

Before her parents even saw that she had entered the room, Caitlin ran to the crib where she found Aden being poked by a dozen or more of the creatures with sharp little sticks. They didn't seem to be harming the boy so much as frightening him.

"Bullies!" Caitlin growled through clenched teeth.

At the sight of her, the monsters shouted in alarm. Armed with their rudimentary weapons, they could do little as Caitlin picked them up one by one and hurled them at the wall as hard as she could. Several fell slack and dead to the floor. The others scurried or limped back into the shadows. At the sight of their fellow rat-men being killed, the other creatures in the room charged at her as she pulled Aden from his crib, ran into the master bathroom, and quickly slammed the door on her Lilliputian enemies.

Gently, she placed Aden in the empty bathtub, grabbed a towel from the rack, and wedged it tightly under the door. If there were monsters in the bathroom, she would deal with them, but Caitlin didn't want any more of them slipping in unnoticed. Once the door was secured, she checked the space for rat creatures but found none. Convinced they were alone, she lifted Aden carefully and talked to him as calmly as she could manage while holding back her own tears.

"I know you're scared, Aden, but these bullies aren't gonna poke you anymore. I won't *let* them. We just gotta get Momma and Daddy out of all that string so we can get out of here."

Aden, of course, could not understand Caitlin's words, but was soothed by her familiar voice as well as the peace taking root in her spirit.

"I can't fight while I'm carrying you, baby brother, so I'm gonna have to put you down. But I'll make sure it's safe. And once I get Momma and Daddy, we'll come get you and we'll *all* be safe. No more pointy sticks, or needles, or monster people. Not *ever*."

She kissed her brother's head repeatedly as she scanned the bathroom. Once she decided where she could hide him, she whispered softly, hoping some part of him could understand.

"I'm gonna put you in the hamper, but you've got to be quiet, Aden. You'll be safe, I promise. You just have to be still and not make any noise while I go save 'em, okay?"

She opened the door to the built-in hamper and saw that there were a few towels and articles of clothing at the bottom. She placed Aden in the center of them and fluffed them up around his sides to try and keep him from rolling over.

"I won't leave you here long," she whispered. "I know those mean ol' things scared you, but I'll teach 'em. Nobody messes with *my* brother. Not bullies. Not monsters. Not *nobody*."

She bent down and kissed his head, then closed the door to the hamper.

She listened for a moment to make sure Aden wouldn't cry, then began to formulate her plan. Outside the bathroom door, the creatures were trying to find a way inside. They had nearly pulled the towel through to their side of the door. It wouldn't hinder their entrance much longer.

Beyond the throng of monsters, her parents were in danger. Caitlin knew that being small didn't mean the creatures couldn't be deadly…especially with her mom and dad captured and restrained. The beasts had purposely struck while everyone was sleeping. They were using their every advantage. To stop them, Caitlin knew she would have to do the same.

Under the bathroom sink, she found the organizer bucket in which her mother stored all the household cleaners. Normally, Caitlin wasn't allowed to touch those things, but there was nothing normal about the young girl's situation, and she firmly believed her mother and father would forgive her for breaking the rules for a good cause.

She read the labels, trying to assess which of the bottles would be of use, but reading and understanding were two different things, and Caitlin didn't comprehend most of what she was reading. One bottle, though, had pictures of scary bugs on it. It had a spray nozzle, so she pulled it out of the bucket and set it aside. Another bottle, not in the organizer but pushed further back under the sink, bore an image of flames next to the microscopic writing on the label. Caitlin understood what *that* symbol meant, so she grabbed it, too.

The speech of the creatures sounded nothing like English, Spanish, or Vietnamese, the three languages Caitlin heard most often in her old neighborhood. The intent behind their words, however, was crystal clear. They wanted in the bathroom. They were after Caitlin and Aden…and they weren't going to stop until they had driven everyone from the house through fear or violence.

Caitlin pondered the tools at her disposal as she searched the drawers of the vanity. In one, she found the pair of scissors her mother always used to trim Aden's hair when it grew long enough to curl. She set those aside and continued her search. Above the toilet, on a floating shelf her father had installed the day before, sat a fat candle that smelled vaguely of berries. Next to it, hidden from Caitlin's view until she stood on the commode, was a small box of matches.

A quick glance back toward the door revealed that the creatures had nearly pulled the towel free from underneath the door. Any moment, they would come streaming into the room with malice and murder in their hearts. The girl knew she had mere seconds to act.

She grabbed the teal bathmat from its position next to the tub and placed it directly in front of the bathroom door. Any creature that entered would have to cross it. She then poured the clear contents of the bottle marked with the flame symbol onto it, soaking every fiber. Caitlin didn't like the way the liquid smelled but, if it did the job she intended for it, she would have no complaint. She broke three matches attempting to get one lit but was finally able to light the candle and step into the bathtub where she would catch her breath until the creatures made the next move.

They didn't keep her waiting long.

As soon as the towel was pulled through to the other side of the door, a mass of the little monsters swarmed under the threshold.

"I'm right here, bullies!" Caitlin shouted. "Come and get me!"

They continued to flood in by the dozens, many of them crossing over the wet bathmat attempting to overtake their target. When the first wave had nearly reached the end of the mat, Caitlin threw the lit candle.

It went out before it hit the bathmat.

A cheer rose from the creatures as they rushed the bathtub. Tiny arrows flew her direction and Caitlin pulled the shower curtain in front of her to block them before leaping from the tub to the toilet where she once again grabbed the box of matches. The creatures on the floor launched another volley and several arrows stuck shallowly in the girl's left side as she struck a match. Unwilling to take any more chances, she hopped over to the vanity and leaned down low and close to the bathmat before dropping the match. She felt the intense blast of heat as dozens of the little beast men went up in flames, squealing as they perished. Those that had pursued Caitlin into the tub stood at its edge looking on in horror as their comrades roasted alive.

Careful to avoid the flames, the girl dropped from the vanity and turned her attention toward the monsters in the tub. She grabbed the bottle of bug spray and doused them all in the solution, hoping it might kill them instantly. Though many shrieked in pain, it did not stop them from launching more arrows and continuing their pursuit. After grabbing the scissors, she opened the bathroom door, ran out, then closed it behind her. At her feet lay the towel the creatures had pulled through. She promptly pushed it back under the door.

Inside her parent's room, many of the monsters were positioned around her mother and father who still struggled against their restraints.

"Close your eyes," she shouted to her parents and then began to pump bug spray onto the creatures, who wailed in surprise as much as pain. While the beasts were distracted, Caitlin used the scissors to cut through the twine binding her father's wrists.

Swatting the creatures within arm's reach, he took the shears and freed himself while Caitlin continued to spray at the ones swarming near her mother. Once loose, her father began attacking their rat-like foes, throwing, punching, and squishing with his bare hands the beasts that had tormented his family.

"Where's Aden?" he asked, slipping his feet into his work boots.

"Bathroom hamper," Caitlin replied.

He handed his daughter the scissors.

"Free your mom. I'm gonna get him."

"There was fire, Daddy. And more bullies. Be careful."

He nodded and then left her there cutting her mother's bonds as he kicked and stomped any creature standing between him and his son.

Once free, Caitlin's mother squeezed her tightly. Wincing, the girl showed her the wounds she had endured during her rescue attempt. Anger twisted her mother's normally kind and lovely face.

"Stay behind me, baby," her mom said. "We're getting out of here."

"There's lots of them. They're *everywhere*."

"You saved us, baby. Now it's Momma's turn to do the saving," her mother replied before shouting, "Frank?"

"I've got him," Caitlin's dad called back. "Just getting the fire out."

"Leave it! Let it burn!"

"This is *our* house. I'm not letting these *things* take it from us."

"We're Godzilla!" Caitlin shouted.

"Damn straight," he said, stepping back into the bedroom with Aden. "But first, we get you guys to safety."

"I'm not leaving you," Teresa said.

"Me neither, Daddy!"

As they spoke, more of the creatures poured in under the bedroom door, launching arrows at the family. Caitlin's mother shielded her from the attack. Her father did the same for baby Aden.

"Get your shoes. Stomping them does wonders," Frank said. "Anything between us and the front door gets squished, kicked, or worse. Once we're outside, we'll figure out how to deal with the rest of them."

"The spray is working," Caitlin said, noting that several that she had doused on the bed now lay dead or dying.

"Then you hang onto that and spray anything that gets close to you and Momma. Aden and I will give them the heel end of my boot."

In the weeks that followed their night of horror, Caitlin struggled to remember how many of the small monsters she and her family had put an end to between her parent's bedroom and the front door downstairs. She only knew that it had been enough. Her father had gone back through the house, removed all the bodies, and thrown them into a fire he built in the backyard. When she asked him why he burned them, her father said something peculiar.

"Because I think a few of them are still in there…watching us," he said, glancing back toward the house. "I want them to remember what we did. And what we're willing to do to anyone who threatens our family."

"We never got the leader that was in my room," Caitlin said. "Do you think he'll come back?"

"I pumped spray insulation into every tiny door, mouse

hole, and crevice I could find, Caiti-bug. If he isn't dead already, I think he and his little rat army will be looking for a new home to call their own. I'm pretty sure he got the message that bullies aren't welcome in our house."

"Or they get stomped hard," Caitlin said.

"Or burned alive. Or sprayed with poison."

"You can't scare Godzilla, right Daddy?"

"That's right. Now, what do you say we take Momma and Aden out to eat at that cool truck stop you guys found? I could go for another pastrami sandwich."

"Eew," Caitlin said, wrinkling her nose. "That's so gross."

CHAPTER 9/
THE EYES AND EVAN RICHMOND

Like most people his age, Evan Richmond had grown up believing there was no limit to his potential. That, with enough work and sheer willpower, he could become anything and anyone he wanted to be. Unlike many others, however, he had enough resources in his corner that it very well might have proven to be true…if not for one unfortunate night.

His parents had conceived him in middle-age and were both quite successful in their chosen careers, thus Evan had lived a life of privilege. Don and Carol Richmond had raised their son to be cunning and stalwart in the pursuit of his goals. What they *could* give him, they did. What they could not, they had little doubt he would earn for himself.

In an age of compelled social awareness, Evan had shied away from their influence and money as he grew into adulthood. His educational path, majoring in Applied Physics, would lead him far from the careers of his parents and, thus, relegate their advice to general life lessons. He wanted to figure things out on his own, work a "joe job" a few hours a week, and sort out his own housing. He wanted a life as open and full of potential as he could manage.

After a strenuous workout the night before, Evan was a bit down in his back the day he moved out of his cramped dormitory (a two-bedroom flat shared by six testosterone-addled men) into a small garage apartment a few blocks from campus. Thankfully, his friend and classmate Gary Dell along with Dell's girlfriend, Dia Palmer, proved more than capable of moving Evan's paltry belongings without his help. Still, he felt bad that they were doing all the heavy lifting and, thus, offered to buy them dinner.

"Are you kidding?" Dia replied, tucking a stray tuft of her brunette hair back into her Broncos cap. "The only thing I've had besides instant ramen all week was when Gary Bear took me out for sliders Wednesday night."

Evan had teased his friend enough about Dia's nickname for him, but he couldn't resist another dig.

"What do you say, Gary Bear? You down for some pizza and beer?"

"Yes, to the pizza. No, to the beer," Gary replied, wiping the sweat from his brow with a bandana he kept in the back pocket of his jeans. "I've got work early in the a.m. and the brewskis tend to make me oversleep. That said, you and Dia aren't 21 yet, pal."

"True," Evan chuckled. "I was just thinking I'd explore the freedom of being off campus is all."

"Another time," Dia assured him. "Now, regarding the pie, are we talking Grazelli's or Sausage 'n' Suds?"

"Sausage 'n' Suds!" both men replied in unison.

"Grazelli's is great for a date night, babe," Gary offered, "but their pizza isn't anything to write home about."

"*I* like it," she said with a faux pout, "but Evan is buying, so whatever. Sausage 'n' Suds is just fine."

"You mind ordering the pies while I help Gary get my bed frame assembled?" Evan asked.

"You sure your back can handle that?" Dia replied. "If *you* call, I can help Gary Bear so you don't risk further injury."

"Oh, sure! As if I'd trust you two anywhere near my bed."

Gary rolled his eyes and said, "Dia won't even let me kiss her in public. If you think she's gonna let me get busy with her in someone else's apartment, you've got another thing coming."

"I'm *so* sorry I'm not a whore," Dia said, sticking out her tongue. "You call for pizza, Evan. And trust me, if Gary lays a hand on me, they'll be able to hear me slap him down at Sausage 'n' Suds…even *without* the phone."

"What's your flavor?" Evan asked with a chuckle.

"Supreme for me," Gary replied.

"Veggie for me," Dia added. "With pineapple."

Both men proceeded to groan in disgust until Dia put her hands on her hips and stared them down.

"The works and a veggie special with fruit," Evan said.

"Got it."

"Since we're setting up your bed," Dia asked, "where will I find your sheets?"

"In the hamper in the corner of the bedroom. You may have to dig for them, though. I washed them with a load of t-shirts and towels and haven't found time to sort them."

"I'll find them," she promised as she followed her boyfriend into the room.

Evan pulled out his cell phone and noticed that he had missed a call from an unknown number. Whoever it was, they had left a voicemail. He ignored it for the time being and kept his attention on the food order.

It was a Thursday night and Sausage 'n' Suds was busy. Though they answered the phone quickly, Evan was immediately asked if he could hold. He agreed and, just as the music began playing, he started getting another call from the unknown number.

"I have no interest in extending my car warranty," he said, not bothering to answer it. "I'd need a car first."

Evan remained on hold for a total of seven minutes and, during that stretch, received two more calls from the unknown number. Each time, he let them go to voicemail. Finally, a pizza employee made it back to the phone and took his order but said that, due to staffing issues, it could be an hour or more before it was delivered.

"Pizza's gonna be a while!" Evan shouted after hanging up. "They're getting slammed tonight."

He was so distracted by the numerous calls from the unknown number that he didn't notice when no reply came from his friends in the bedroom. He wanted to check those voicemails.

He clicked on the first one, which he had missed some 45 minutes earlier when he and his friends had been in the middle of moving stacks of boxes from the garage area up to the apartment. He prepared himself for a well-scripted sales pitch. Instead, he got a garbled and static-filled message from a young man who sounded desperate.

"Mr. Richmond, w*sssskkkkkkkkk* met. My na*sssskkkk-kkkkk* Drake and what I'm abo*sssskkkkkkkkk* strange if *sssskkkkkkkkkk*tely idiotic, but it's imperative that you l*ssssk-kkkkk* new apartment as soon as possi*sssskkkkkkkkk* not, under *sssskkkkkkkkk*, let yo*sssskkkkkkk* Gary and Dia go in th*sssskkkkkkkkkkk*en you get somewhe*sssskkkkkkkkk* back at 817-5*sssskkkkkkkk*ase, Mr. Richmond. You are all in grav*sssskkkkkkkkkk*ut of that apartment."

Evan stared at his phone for a moment before clicking the next message.

"Mr. Richmo*sssskkkkkkkkk*Dylan Dra*sssskkkkkkkkkk*on my way to you as *sssskkkkkkkk*n't possibly make it in time for your fr*sssskkkkkkkk*st save them yourself. Do *sssskkkkk-kkkk*nce, let Gary Dell and Dia Palm*sssskkkkkkkkkkkkkk-kkk*omething there. Something evil th*sssskkkkk*ts nothing mo*sssssskkkkkk*stroy your lives. Please, Evan, *sssssssskkkkkk-kkk*nsane. Call me a *sssssskkkkkkk*ever makes you feel *ssskk-kkkkkkk*n't let your frien*sssssssskkkkkkk*to that room."

"Guys, you should come hear this," Evan shouted. "Some weirdo is spamming my phone. See if you recognize his voice. He's gotta be a Lamba Delt or someone from the Drama Department having a laugh."

He put his phone on speaker mode, hoping it would allow his friends to hear in the other room as he clicked the third voicemail.

"Mr. Richmo*sssssssskkkkkkkkkkk* my previous messages and did *ssssskkkkkkkk*ed, *ssssssskkkkkkkkkk*ot, I'm afraid Mr. Dell and Miss Palmer are already dea*sssssskkkkkkkkk*ur world is about to be upside down. It shouldn't ha*ssssssssss-kkkkk* I should've reached you in ti*sssssskkkkkkkkkkkkkk-kkk*as gone wrong. Someone is actively work*sssssssskkkkk-kkkkkk*one who doesn't want me to interfe*sssskkkkkkk* your friends are alive or dead, Evan, you need to get *sssssssk-kkkkkkkkk*ment. Don't *ssssssskkkkkkkk* evil that's lurking there. I'm sendi*ssssskkkkkk*d. He's coming. H*sssskkkkkk* tight."

Evan was not a particularly superstitious young man. The world had plenty of genuine evil in it without believing in the supernatural. Who needed ghosts, monsters, and vampires when you had greedy corporations, climate change, and the recent pandemic to contend with? Still, the stranger's warning and the tone of his voice struck a chord deep inside

Evan that he couldn't ignore. He found himself hesitant to listen to the fourth message.

"Hey, guys?" he called out. "Could you hear that in there?"

When no answer came, Evan felt a chill somewhere in his core. It wasn't that they hadn't responded to him, but that he could hear no sounds coming from the room in general. And when had they closed the door?

"Gary? Dia? Could you hear that in the bedroom?"

He stood, though his back protested, and stared at the door to the bedroom a moment before trying a bit louder.

"Gary? Dia?"

As he approached the door slowly, he clicked on the 4th message.

"Evan, if you didn't keep them from going into *sssssskkk-kkkkk* too late. There's nothing to be *ssskkkkksssskkkkk*here. The Eyes want you, too, Evan. You mus*sssskkkkkkk*ay from that door. You can't save them. You ca*ssskkkkkk*save your-self."

But Evan couldn't stay away. His friends were in there, weren't they? No cryptic warning was going to convince a physics major that some unforeseen evil with a capital 'E' was making dinner of his friends. Those sorts of things didn't happen. At least, that's what Evan believed until he opened the bedroom door.

Still holding tightly to the doorknob, he gazed past the

frame and into what should have been his modest bedroom with its window that overlooked the neighbor's willow tree. Instead of his four off-white walls, his full-sized bed, and the bureau he had purchased at a garage sale the weekend prior, all Evan could see beyond the door frame was a blackness so deep and rich that it drove all sources of light from the room.

"Gary?"

At the sound of his friend's name, something appeared in the darkness near the center of the room, but Evan couldn't process what he was seeing.

"Dia?"

"Gary? Dia?" a voice returned to him, mocking the worry in Evan's tone.

It was at the sound of the voice that the young man realized what it was he saw there in the pitch black of his room: eyes, red and malevolent, seemingly floating in the center of a void. Fear gripped Evan with such ferocity that every muscle in his body seized at once. He couldn't summon the will to let go of the doorknob let alone run for his life.

"You are all the same, Evan Richmond," the voice said, the mocking timbre it previously held now replaced with acidic contempt. "Always so brave and carefree until your eyes are opened to the deep and terrifying strangeness of your world, filled with horrors you can scarcely imagine. And your world, boy, is but one of *many*. Multiply your insignificance by infinity and despair. Hope is a child's fantasy…a game you've already lost. And faith is as dead as your Gary and Dia."

Evan felt the hot tears running down his face. He could taste them at the corners of his lips. His every instinct was to run and to keep running until he reached the end of the world. His own death was a hair's breadth away, and he wept because he knew *nothing* could save him from whatever awful fate awaited him in the void of his room.

But Evan was wrong.

The sound of breaking glass came from beyond the darkness and suddenly light pierced the heart of it, prompting a feral scream from the Eyes within the void. Though momentarily blinded by the light, the young man could make out the form of a stranger battling with shadow-like creatures threatening to overwhelm him and extinguish the source of light he held in one hand. In the stranger's other fist was a sword and, with it, he cleaved the shadows in two. The man wore a strange cloak and spoke words that Evan couldn't understand.

As he watched the battle unfold before him, Evan realized his body was no longer frozen with fright. As if reading his mind, the swordsman shouted for Evan to run. And run he did. Out of the apartment. Down the block. Across the university grounds. And all the way to the campus security department, where he collapsed in tears.

As he told the police what had happened to him, Evan knew they didn't believe him. Not about the Eyes nor the man with the sword who had saved his life. And later, when they showed him horrific photos of Gary and Dia eviscerated and posed like some mockery of Michelangelo's Pietà, the devastated young man knew he would soon be charged with their murders.

His trial made the national news. The young man's attorneys pled insanity despite Evan maintaining his innocence. Even after they were anonymously sent a news clipping about a similar murder in California, they refused to entertain a plea of not guilty. Like Evan, the woman convicted of the 2007 murder of Sean Mathers claimed to have seen "red eyes" in the darkness of the room, a phenomenon she had previously experienced at the scene of her father's suicide. The attorneys assured him that the prosecution would argue Evan had read about the Corrine Mathers trial and concocted a similar story in a weak effort to create reasonable doubt. No jury would buy into the notion of a supernatural serial killer.

Prosecution had done their best to paint the young defendant as a sociopath, going so far as to suggest that his wealthy parents had paid the counselor and other staff members at Evan's private high school to keep his mental health issues quiet. That they had knowingly turned a blind eye to their son's rage. Their unwillingness to treat his mental health issues, they argued, had led to a psychotic break and, ultimately, to the untimely deaths of two university students whose only crime had been befriending the ticking time bomb named Evan Richmond.

After many months of trial and deliberation, Evan was found guilty of the involuntary manslaughter of Gary Dell and Dia Palmer by reason of insanity. He was sentenced to 20 years in a state psychiatric facility upstate. Evan's parents were naturally distraught. They tried to visit several times, but their son had no desire to see them. Like everyone else, they believed Evan had lost his mind and killed his friends in a gruesome fashion. What could he possibly have to say to them?

A fter nearly 3 months in the facility, Evan had another visitor: a reporter, according to an orderly, who wanted to hear more about what the young man claimed to have seen that deadly night, but Evan refused to see him.

That same evening, Evan was awakened from a sound sleep by a strong hand on his shoulder. He opened his eyes to find a stranger, certainly no older than Evan's own 19 years, seated at the edge of his cot.

"I'm sorry to frighten you," the stranger said, "but you left me little choice. When you wouldn't see me this afternoon, I had to get creative."

"The reporter?" Evan asked.

"That was a bit of pretense," the man replied. "It seems

they won't allow just anyone in to visit and I'm too young for them to believe I'm an attorney or a doctor."

"I know your voice," Evan said, sitting up straight. "I *heard* your voice on the phone that night!"

"Yes, yes. Now quiet down, Mr. Richmond, or you'll get me thrown out of here."

Evan looked the stranger over. He was dressed casually in jeans and a pale green t-shirt. Over it, he wore a brown cotton blazer with a pin on his lapel that read: Shine On. Though his face was young and unblemished, his kind eyes seemed much older and more resolute if not a bit sad.

"You called me," Evan said softly, "and tried to warn me about…the Eyes."

"That I did. I'm so sorry I was too late."

"Who *are* you?"

"That's a bit of a complicated question. And, like my voicemails, I fear you'd have a hard time believing most of it."

"I learned my lesson. You tell me the truth, buddy, and I'll believe you...no matter how crazy it sounds."

The stranger smiled sadly at that.

"The creature that killed your friends was not of this world, Evan. It was a supernatural being from a reality wholly separate from your own. I don't know how it managed to cross into your reality. I *do* know that your friends weren't its first victims."

"That woman in Cali," Evan whispered.

"Corrine Mathers, yes. It killed her father and then, many years later, came back for her husband. So far as I've been able to tell, there's little rhyme or reason to it. No pattern. Only chaos, fear, and death up and down this timeline."

"Let's back up to the bit where you said it came from another reality. Are we talking multiverses? Parallel realities?"

The stranger rubbed his hairless chin and thought.

"I appreciate that your love of physics gives you a frame of reference for such things, Mr. Richmond," he said, "but a simple 'yes' would an oversimplification. The greater truth is far too vast for any textbook to ever make sense of it. My only understanding of it comes from experiencing it first-hand."

"You aren't from this reality either? What exactly are you, then?"

The stranger chuckled at that.

"A man, I assure you. No more or less so than you, Mr. Richmond. Like the terrible evil you encountered that night, I come from a place beyond this reality of yours…though quite similar in many aspects. I've been tasked with setting right any deviations from the intended narrative."

"Intended by whom?"

"The Author of all things."

"That sounds...religious. I don't believe in any of that," Evan said. "The only one deciding my fate is me."

The stranger smiled and sighed.

"I once thought the same. And, certainly, our free will influences our narratives. Such was written into us from the start. But behind it all, our stories are written into being and, sometimes, what was meant to be is altered in such a way that damage could be done to a great many souls and their stories."

"For the sake of argument, let's say that's true. Why would this author of yours allow such things to happen?"

"As I said, we are creatures of free will. We often change the path our narratives might have taken. By doing so, we may run into danger or avoid great blessings that awaited us had we stayed on the path we were made for. The being you faced that night, the murderer of your friends, has set his own will toward disrupting as many narratives as possible."

"What was that thing? And why did it come for me?"

"I'm not entirely certain on either count. I believe, though, that a sub-creator, someone with the power to create lesser narratives of their own, must have found a way to free the monster from its own story and unleash it upon this unsuspecting world."

"I...I-m sorry. I still don't really understand."

"I know. Even if I had the time to explain it fully, it would be a bit beyond the pale for you without seeing all that I've seen."

"Then why did you come here?"

"To apologize for starters. I entered your world attempting to save you. I should have arrived near enough to you to intervene, to defend you and your friends, but everything went wrong. Something or someone interfered with my arrival, and I joined your tale too far away to reach you in time."

"That's why you called," Evan said.

"That's why I called, yes. And even in that, I failed."

"Your messages were mostly static. I could only make out bits and pieces. I thought you were just a crank."

"I've come to believe that whoever interfered with my arrival likewise hindered my attempts to reach you by phone."

"Someone was there, though," Evan said. "A man with a bright light. And a sword, I think."

"That was my mentor. He is the other reason I've come. When I realized I was being thwarted, I sent word for him to intervene. He's been at this quite a bit longer than I have, and I had hoped he could do what I couldn't."

"He saved my life. Kept that thing busy long enough for me to run."

"For which I'm grateful, but I was hoping you could shed some light on what happened to him afterward. He's been out of communication since that night and, even with all the resources at my disposal, I've been unable to locate him."

"He was battling that *thing*. That's the last I saw of him. He told me to run, and I did."

"And he's made no effort to contact you since?"

"No."

The stranger appeared worried. Despite his young features, his bearing suggested a maturity and wisdom beyond anything Evan had ever seen in someone his own age.

"If the Eyes were real," Evan said, "then you can find a way to prove it, right? You can get me out of here?"

The young stranger placed his hand on Evan's shoulder.

"Mr. Richmond, I cannot help but feel partially responsible for your predicament. Had things worked the way there were meant to, I would have reached you and your friends before more blood was spilled. But, in this world, supernatural things do not exist apart from the original creative work of the Author. That creature forced its way here from somewhere *else*. For all I know, my friend and the Eyes destroyed each other right there in your apartment. I can no more prove to anyone that it existed than you could prove Frodo Baggins existed…because its existence did not originate in this place."

"You mean I'm stuck here?"

"For the time being. It is certainly not my intention for you to pay for a crime you didn't commit. That was not the way your narrative was meant to play out. But whatever breach allowed this monster through has already altered your story in a way that I cannot easily repair. The best I could do at *this* point would be to break you out of here, but then you'd be forced to spend your life on the run."

"No offense," Evan said, "but that sounds a bit better than spending the next 20 years in *this* place."

"I hesitate because I cannot foresee all ends. The interference that kept me from arriving at your side that night was clearly meant to thwart my purpose in this tale. Why? Is someone bent toward your destruction or were you merely the means used to attack the purpose of the Author and His work? If you are the target, what is to be gained from altering your destiny? Why remove you from the narrative path you were already on? What is the endgame?"

"You lost me."

"Never mind all that. If I were to set you free, Mr. Richmond, your life might be in greater danger. Perhaps you are safe in this institution simply because you are far afield of whatever path your freedom would set you on. Since the attempt on your life failed, you were removed from the equation by landing here."

"But you don't know that for certain," Evan argued.

"No. I'm afraid I don't."

"It's a risk I'm willing to take."

"I'm certain it is," the stranger replied sadly. "But it's not one that I *will* take. I won't have more blood on my hands. I need to know what caused this breach, Mr. Richmond. I need to understand *how* this happened. That will require time and investigation. Only when I can be sure that I am not setting you up for failure or death, that I am not playing into my enemy's hands, will I be willing to set you loose in the world. Until then, I believe you are safer here."

"That's not fair," Evan said, the tension in his voice twisting his features.

"There's no such thing as fair. There's only what is and what isn't. But I agree with you that it isn't *just*. I won't leave you here long-term, but for now there is simply nowhere safer for you to be."

Evan nodded, a tear or two dripping from his chin.

"Once I locate my mentor, we'll see to it that the threat to your life is well and truly over and return for you. Until then, hold fast to hope."

"Hope is a child's fantasy. A game you've already lost. And faith is as dead as Gary and Dia," Evan mumbled, his head in his hands.

"Pardon?"

"It's what the Eyes said just before your friend arrived and saved me…if you call *this* saving."

"Perhaps that's a clue," the young stranger replied. "If

that creature sought to drive hope from you…or to kill your sense of faith, it may have been with good reason. Perhaps your path would've led you into conflict with the beast or whomever is pulling its strings. As I said earlier, it may have been trying to remove some opposition from the playing field. I won't know for certain until I've researched further."

"And I'll just rot here in the meantime?"

"Hopefully not for long. One way or another, we'll see this made right. Or at least as right as it can be considering your circumstances."

"What if I don't make it?" Evan asked, his voice trembling. "What if this place, o-or the memory of what happened to my friends, breaks me?"

The stranger reached out and put his hand on Evan's sternum.

Though he had been raised not to believe in the supernatural, his encounter with the Eyes had changed Evan's understanding of what was possible. The creature had spoken of the depths of horror that most were blissfully unaware of, and the murder of his friends had convinced Evan of that reality. It left him feeling small, weak, and filled with a dread that his subsequent trial and sentencing had only underscored. Since his imprisonment, every breath had felt like a struggle…some futile attempt to stay alive in a world where all was lost.

At the stranger's touch, Evan began to weep and tremble

as if the weight of the world had suddenly fallen from his shoulders. He made no attempt to hide his tears as the young stranger spoke.

"May the Author of our stories give you peace. May His grace be a light in the darkest gloom and may the hope of His promises become an endless wellspring for your soul."

"Who are you?" Evan asked, brushing his tears away with the back of his hand.

"A friend. My name is Dylan Drake…and I'll be back for you, Evan. That is my promise."

After the young man left his room, Evan relaxed his face and cursed beneath his breath. He followed the curse by ripping his pillow to shreds and watching the feathers drift around the room on the minimal current provided by the hospital's overtaxed HVAC system.

Atop the cot in the other corner of the room, completely shrouded in shadow, a figure sat upright. Her laugh was as cruel as it was melodic. When she stopped and swung her legs over the side of the bed, Evan could feel her eyes sizing him up.

"Is it not exactly as I said?" she asked. "They will never share their power, Evan. They've left you in this hole to wither, far removed from all you could attain. Content to play the hero in someone else's story while your destiny is usurped by lesser men."

Evan bit his bottom lip until it bled, rocking in his bed as she stood and approached him.

"This Dylan Drake is a liar," she said, placing one pale hand on his shoulder. "But now that I know his *name,* he can be dealt with. Rest assured that he will pay for his interference…along with that pathetic display of false compassion he tried to sell you. Your tears were a nice touch, by the way. *Very* convincing."

"And the other one? The mentor?"

"He'll come for you. Eventually. Until then, you train. You learn. About him. About his Master. And even about the wizard in their back pocket. Then, when the time is right…"

"…I'll kill them," Evan said, leaning into her touch. "I'll kill them all. Just for you."

CHAPTER 10/
SMILE

ndrea Kent was badly hungover. The wedding rehears-
al and post-rehearsal dinner for the Johns-Wagner nup-
tials had run early into the morning and the drinks had been
plentiful and strong. After a grotesque offering to the por-
celain gods and an all-too-brief nap, she had managed to
drag herself to the wedding venue to get ready for the big
event.

Just north of Napa Valley, the picturesque winery sat amid
acres of vines and a parcel of Heritage Oak trees. Hair and
makeup were being done in the adjacent historic carriage
house replete with its cathedral ceilings and intricate wood-
work crafted by Italian artisans some 120 years earlier.

Andrea, however, barely noticed the breathtaking nature
of her surroundings as she dropped into the makeup chair
with a thud, doing her best not to vomit again.

"God, Andy," her friend and fellow bridesmaid, Danielle
Montez, said with a smirk. "You look worse than I do…and
I feel like every single level of hell settled into my skull and
played the anvil chorus on my retinas."

"Descriptive," Andrea grumped. "Thanks, Dani."

"You were knocking back shots like I've never seen, Andy," Fiona Akins chimed in. "I think Sarah's dad finally dragged you out of there around 4 a.m. after the bar called upstairs and woke him and Mrs. J out of a sound sleep."

"Shit. Why didn't you guys pull me out sooner?"

"Girl, I was wasted as *fuck*," Dani replied. "I was gone long before that. Brad pulled me upstairs and threw me in a cold shower to sober me up."

"Did it work?" Fiona asked.

"It pissed me off," Dani replied. "But being pissed is pretty damn sobering. So, I took some ibuprofen and hit the hay. Now *he's* pissed that he didn't get laid."

"I'm sure you'll make it up to him tonight. Anyone seen Sara yet?"

Andrea shook her head.

"Haven't seen the blushing bride," Dani confirmed. "She ducked out early last night like a good girl. She'll be the perfectly beautiful bride today and we'll all look like warmed-over dog shit. She should be *glad* we got wasted. It'll just make her look better."

"Speak for yourself, Montez," Fiona replied. "I look damn good, and I only had two drinks last night."

Before Dani could reply, the makeup artist entered the room and assessed the damage. As she began to work on

Fiona, the hairdresser arrived to start styling Andrea, who was happy to close her eyes and let the woman work. She rested comfortably until Fiona kicked her lightly in the shin.

"What the hell, Fi?"

"You were asleep, girl. And she was asking you a question."

Andrea looked up at the hairdresser and smiled weakly.

"Sorry," she offered. "I'm still feeling the aftereffects of a long night of...tequila, mostly."

"It's okay, dear," the hairdresser said. She was a plump, older woman whose faint South African accent reminded Andrea of an actress whose name she couldn't quite recall. "I was just asking if you want this bit curled. Or should I pin it up like this?"

She demonstrated her intention and the other two bridesmaids seemed to approve.

"You sold us," Andrea said. "Pin it." She then turned to Dani and asked, "Anything from the star of the show while I dozed?"

"Sara's got her own team of magic workers in the room next door," Dani replied. "She texted and said she'd meet up with us when it's time to dress."

"Speaking of magic workers," Fiona said, "what was with the guy you were talking to at the bar last night, Kent?"

"Yeah," Dani chimed in. "What was his deal?"

Andrea looked at them blankly, trying to recall the night before. It remained a haze.

"Come on," Fiona said, leaning forward and clearly frustrating the makeup artist. "You can't tell me that you're too hungover to remember *that* guy. He was all over you and you seemed to be eating it up. Mr. J said he practically had to pry you away from him."

"Really? I know I was pretty wasted but…I have no memory of talking to anyone last night. What'd he look like?"

"Kind of handsome in a creepy, stoned Johnny Depp sort of way," Dani offered. "The one time I walked over to the bar from where Brad and I were seated, he was telling you all this dark nonsense about fate and passing the consequences of your actions off onto others. Weird philosophical bullshit, you know? I've had dudes say plenty of strange things to try to get in *my* pants over the years—"

"And most of it worked," Fiona added.

"Fuck you very much, Fi," Dani said sharply before continuing. "I've heard my share of pitches, you know? But your guy was talking voodoo or some occult shit. If he hadn't been on the verge of hot, you'd have surely sent him packing."

"I don't remember any of it," Andrea confessed. "Was he staying in the hotel?"

"Who the hell knows?"

"He creeped me out, Andy," Fiona admitted. "If you *do* bump into him again, steer clear. Ain't no man alive worth making a deal with the devil for."

Dani laughed so hard she snorted. Andrea laughed, too, but tried not to disrupt the work being done on her hair.

"Laugh all you want," Fiona said. "That dude had a bad vibe. I'm glad Mr. J chased him off and pulled you out of there, Andy. Trust me. He saved you from a world of trouble."

"The *tequila* was trouble," Dani corrected. "The dude was just trying to be edgy so he could get a taste of what our Andy was putting out on the table."

"Shut up," Andrea said, kicking at Dani playfully. "Whoever he was, he's gone. And not a worry."

Once the hairdresser was done with Andy, the hungover bridesmaid switched to the makeup chair and tried to be still while the cosmetics artist, a young Latino woman named Destiny, attempted to mask a few of the more noticeable effects of her hangover.

Once Andy's makeup was finished, she left while the work continued on Fiona and Dani. Next door, she found the bride, Sara Johns, and her younger sister and maid-of-honor, Macy, being worked on by a team of their own.

"*Ho-ly* shit," Macy said with a smirk at the sight of her. "Looks like I lost the bet, sis. Kent actually dragged her ass out of bed and made it."

"Leave her alone," the bride warned. "You don't want to piss Andy off when she's this hungover. Trust me. I nearly lost a tooth once."

"Haw-haw-haw," Andrea said, rolling her eyes. "The Johns sisters, folks. Entertaining the masses with their humor since...well, *never* basically."

"You look good," Sara replied. "They did a great job hiding those puffy eyes you're sporting. Did you at least get laid? Dad said he had to chase off some creep at the bar."

"So I was told. Can't remember any of it, sadly."

"You were skunked," Macy said, wrinkling her nose. "Daddy said the guy was a total douchebag. Even after he told him to get lost, the scuzzball kept trying to whisper in your ear in some sort of weirdo moon language. Just couldn't take a damn clue."

"I feel bad that Mr. Johns got called down on my account. I plan to apologize profusely when I see him."

"He didn't mind," Sara said. "Do you have any idea how many times he gets a call from Monster Macy in some sort of trouble?"

"Oh, fuck off," Macy said. "I'm not the one he had to bail out of *jail*."

"I was marching for a good cause!"

"Are your folks mad at me?" Andrea asked.

"Nah, you're good," Sara assured her. "It was a rough year

for everyone. Dad knows you were just blowing off some steam and getting a bit lost in the celebration. He was young once. He remembers what it was like. Even Mom, prude that she is, was more worried about you than angry. You're fine."

"You look gorgeous, by the way," Andrea said. "Macy, too."

"But not as good as me, right?"

"No. Not even remotely."

"Does Barry Manilow know that you raid his wardrobe?" Macy replied. When her sister and Andrea cocked their eyebrows in response, she sighed. "Come on, you barbarians! *The Breakfast Club!* It's an 80's classic!"

"Nerd," Andrea replied.

"Dweeb," followed Sara.

"All finished," the hairstylist working on the bride proclaimed, spinning her around to see it in the mirror.

"I love it," Sara said. "You're a miracle worker, Michelle. Thank you. Do you mind taking a photo of Andy and I?"

The hairdresser agreed and took Sara's phone to snap the photo. Andrea bent down so the bride could remain seated and put her head as close as she dared to her friend's without risking either of their hairdos. It hurt to smile, but Andrea managed until the flash caused a sharp spike of pain to shoot through her head.

"Shit!"

"Poor baby," Sara said, offering a kind smile. "Need something for that headache?"

"I took something already," Andrea replied. "It was just the flash. Send me that pic, would you?"

"Sure, hon," she said, texting the photo before she could forget. "We've got a few minutes before everyone is ready to start getting dressed. If you want to lay down—"

Andrea shook her head.

"I don't want to mess up my hair or the makeup. I'll be fine. I just need to make it through the next few hours. You've got the harder job."

"Please," Macy scoffed. "I've got the *hardest* job. All the stress of a wedding without the husband to show for it."

"Stop being a raging bitch for half a second and you might catch one," Sara said, winking at Andrea.

"I'm choosing to be nice today," Macy said, pointing a finger in warning. "But don't *push* me."

It wasn't until she realized that Andrea wasn't laughing with her that Sara knew something was wrong. The bridesmaid's face was pale as she stared at her phone.

"What's wrong, Andy?"

"The photo," Andrea said, turning her phone to show Sara. "Look."

"What am I looking at? Are you worried about those

bags? Because I really don't think anyone will notice from a distance, sweety. You look great!"

"No. M-my smile. Look at my smile."

"What about it?"

"Don't you see it? It's…wrong. Distorted or something."

Sara looked confused. Putting her thumb and pointer finger on the screen and spreading them apart, she zoomed in on Andrea Kent's face.

"It looks fine to me. I'm not sure what you mean."

But it did not look *fine* to Andrea. To her, the grin was all wrong. Like someone else was smiling back at her.

"She's gonna hurl," Macy predicted. "Get a bucket or something."

"No, I'm fine," Andrea insisted.

"Fine? You're as pale as a ghost, Andy," Sara said. "If you aren't going to lie down, at least *sit*. I don't want you passing out on me."

"Mom and Dad are in the ballroom keeping an eye out for early guests," Macy offered. "Dad's probably got some old-fashioned hangover remedy he can have the bartender whip up for you."

"I'm fine, Macy. I'm just a bit—"

"Fractured?"

Andrea turned to see that Fiona was finished with her hair and makeup and was poking her head into the room from the hallway outside.

Before giving Andrea a chance to reply, she added, "Damn, Sara Johns, you clean up shinier than a new penny!"

"Thanks, Fi!" Sara replied joyfully. "You look great, too."

"Montez is nearly done," Fiona reported. "She asked me to come see how close we are to getting dressed."

"I'd say 20 minutes or so," Macy offered. "Don't want big sis sweating it out too long. That dress is pretty, but—"

"It's not very comfortable," Sara finished. "Plus, because it's strapless, I kind of have to be taped into it to keep the girls in line. Can't have every dude in attendance getting a peek at Stuart's private show."

"Please," Macy scoffed. "As if *some* of those guys haven't beaten Stu Wagner to the buffet."

"You're gross," Sara said, ignoring the fact that Fiona chuckled at Macy's comment. "Fi, can you take Andy to sit down somewhere and drink some water. She won't listen to *me*, and I don't want her keeling over when she's shuffle-stepping down the aisle on Walt Peirero's arm."

"On it, boss," Fiona said, giving her a half-hearted salute. She then turned to Andrea and prompted, "Come on, zombie girl, let's get some color in you."

Fiona Akins dragged her hungover friend out of the room

and into the ballroom where the two wedding planners were busy putting the finishing touches on the venue's decorations. One of them had the Mother and Father of the Bride engaged in conversation near the front of the room as Fiona approached the other, who was busy straightening chairs at the back.

"I'm sorry to bother you," Fiona said, "but I've got a bridesmaid here in need of some TLC after a long night of debauchery. Do you know where I can get her some water?"

"The room next door is already set up for the reception," the planner, a thirty-something with short-cropped hair said dryly. "So long as you don't touch anything, you can take her in there. Bartender is already set up and has sodas and waters on offer."

"Thanks," Fiona replied, dragging Andrea along.

"Fi, this is silly. I'm *fine*."

"You're as white as paste, Kent. Even worse than when Montez and I were busting your balls in the makeup chair."

"But it's not the hangover," Andrea insisted, handing her friend her phone. "It's this."

Fiona looked at the photo of two of her closest friends and then back to Andrea.

"I don't get it."

"What do you see?"

"You and Johns all dolled up and ready to shine. Why?"

"But my smile…don't you see it?"

"Yeah. So? I've seen you smile thousands of times, crazy pants."

"Not like *this*. It's wrong. It's—"

"It's what?" Fiona asked, clearly confused.

"I don't know how to explain it. If I didn't know better, I'd say someone else's smile was edited onto my face…which is, admittedly, crazy."

"I know my share of crazy people, Kent, and you ain't one of them. You're just feeling the aftereffects of a rough night. We aren't getting any younger, you know. You overestimated your ability to hang, that's all. Live and learn. Now let's get you that water. Or maybe some juice. The bar is bound to have something citrusy."

"Yes, please," Andrea replied, managing a smile.

A few minutes later, as she sat quietly sipping on an orange juice in the reception area, Nathan and Pamela Johns entered. As the Mother of the Bride worked her way to the bar to discuss something with the bartender, Mr. Johns made a beeline for Fiona and Andrea. As he approached, his features softened with concern.

"Andrea, are you alright?" he asked. "Pam and I were quite worried about you last night."

"I'm very sorry," Andrea offered. "I don't normally drink so much, Mr. Johns. I just lost track of the time and the number of drinks and…I feel really embarrassed they woke you up to come get me."

"Nonsense," he said, dismissing the notion with a wave of his hand. "I had given the bartender my number for just such a situation, dear. You needn't be embarrassed. I was less worried about the drinks than the company you were keeping."

"I'm afraid I don't remember that. Sara said he was creepy."

"Sara is a master of understatement. I'm a retired marine colonel, young lady, as you well know, and that man gave *me* pause. There was something sinister at work behind his eyes as he was sizing me up. I can admit I felt relieved when he took my threat seriously and vacated the bar."

"That's not my *usual* type, I promise."

"Again, no need for apologies. He likely latched onto you after you'd already had one too many. I did take a photo of him, though, in case he caused you any trouble. He didn't like being on camera at all. Acted like a trapped animal."

"Can I see him?" Fiona asked.

"Of course," he said, fishing for his phone.

"Why?" Andrea asked.

"Because Mr. Johns is a badass," Fiona replied. "Anyone dumb enough to even *think* of tangling with him is someone I want to steer clear of. I need a better look at this guy."

"I don't think he'll be a problem anymore," Nathan Johns

said as he turned his phone around for them to see. "But if he's staying at our hotel, it might be best to avoid him. And, of course, you have my number if you need me to intervene."

"Thanks Mr. Johns," Fiona said, before noticing the look on her friend's face. "What is it, Kent? You remember him now?"

"No," Andrea answered, finding it difficult to breathe. "It's that smile. His smile. It's—"

"Cocky," Mr. Johns offered. "I'm telling you, before the flash went off, he seemed like he wanted to tussle. Maybe he was so pickled the bright light disoriented him."

"His smile is all *wrong* somehow," Andrea said. "Like it's not—"

"Not what?"

"I don't know. Not human."

"He may have been a weasel, Andrea, but he was most definitely human," Mr. Johns said. "I'm just glad I got there when I did. I think he was trying to take you out of there when I arrived."

"Macy said something about him whispering in another language?"

"I didn't recognize it," the older man admitted. "But it *was* disturbing. Like something you'd see in one of those scary films, Pam and the girls like so much. The kind of nonsense you'd hear black-robed occultists chanting to wake the devil or something equally ridiculous. I'm certain it was bullshit, Andrea, but I didn't really want him in your ear."

"Or in your anything else," Fiona chuckled.

"Fiona, please. There's no need to be vulgar. Especially on such a celebratory day." He put his phone away and added, "You two are due out back in about ten minutes for pre-wedding photos."

"We'll be there," Andrea assured him.

"Good. And, Andrea, try not to worry. You've got a lot of friends around you today. And Pam and I consider you girls to be an extension of our family. If trouble rears its head, we've got your back. Always."

Andrea stood and kissed Mr. Johns on the cheek.

Fiona followed it with a hug. Once he was gone, her smile disappeared as she glanced back over to her longtime friend.

"You're worried. And it's *not* about embarrassing yourself in front of Mr. and Mrs. J. So why does this creep from the bar have you so up in your own head?"

"I don't know," Andrea admitted. "I just feel an overwhelming sense of dread. Something is wrong that I can't put my finger on."

"You're hungover, dipshit. You drank too much, didn't get laid, and have a whole day ahead of you in which you're expected to make the occasion as perfect as possible for one of your best friends. We're all feeling the pressure."

"Maybe you're right, Fi."

"I'm *always* right. Now finish that juice so we can get dressed and prop you up for some photos."

"Joy."

After the wedding, as people milled about the reception hall, Andrea sat with an untouched plate of food, staring at the photo she had taken with the bride. That damned smile—'No, not damned,' Andrea thought. '*Demonic.*'—was still haunting her. She had tried to put it out of her mind, but every photo she had been forced to smile for had made her feel like she was losing herself to madness.

The rest of the wedding party was enjoying the festivities, but Andrea found it difficult to force any more smiles. Soon the table was filled with laughter and stories and she began to feel like an anchor around their necks. Sara had noticed but was thankfully too distracted to say anything. Macy, though, had kicked the bridesmaid under the table and raised her eyebrows, clearly code for: What the hell is wrong with you, Andy?

"Excuse me," Andrea said, pushing back from the table.

"You okay?" The bride asked.

"Still a bit wobbly. I thought some fresh air might cure

what ails me."

"I'll come with," Dani offered.

"No, it's fine. I won't be a minute."

The fresh air did provide a brief respite. The grapevines were not yet ready for harvest, and the vineyard was far enough away from the cities and interstates that there was no traffic noise to grate on the nerves and no light pollution to lessen the magnificence of the stars. It was the perfect venue for a wedding, and she honestly hoped Sara would be happy with her life to come.

Andrea was so lost in her momentary relief from worry that she didn't hear the footsteps approaching until it was too late.

"Smile."

She turned to see him there, grinning like a devil, holding out his phone. The man from the bar. The man Nathan Johns thought he had scared away. His wicked smile, however, revealed that there was no fear within him. Only ill intent.

The flash blinded her for a moment and sent a chill through the length of her body.

"Took me a while to find you," he said softly. His voice sounded old and strange, as if multiple voices were being blended into one but couldn't quite synch up.

"Leave me alone," she said, trying to blink away her blindness.

"Oh, Andrea, it's too *late* for that, I'm afraid. It was already too late when that old bastard started pushing me around last night. The work was already done."

"Work?"

"Passing off my burdens...and the awful consequences riding along in their sidecar."

Her eyes began to clear, and she could almost make out his shape. She was prepared to run or scream, but his flash went off again and pain shot through her head, doubling her over.

"I'd have thought a day like this would've done the job. So many photos to take. So many flashes going off. Pulling pieces of you away to store them on a memory card...as if we aren't fragmented enough already."

"Leave me alone," she demanded, hating how weak the words sounded as they passed her lips. "Why are you doing this?"

"Well, for one thing, it's fun. I know you can't understand that. You normies are so caught up in your rules and laws that you can't even *imagine* the freedom of not giving a shit. Second, once you drunkenly told me about the wedding you were going to be part of, I couldn't pass up the chance to try out my little spell in a more public venue."

"Spell?"

"Spell. Recipe. Mind trick. *Suggestion.* Whatever you'd like to call it, girl."

He took another photo, blinding her with the flash.

It hurt so badly that Andrea heard herself hiss and growl at him like a wounded animal.

"*There* you are," the man said with a laugh. "Come out and play already. Let's see what sort of trouble you can get up to. Just a few more pictures now, Andrea. Smile for me."

Andrea felt the urge to curse at him. She wanted to run. To fight. But she found she no longer had that much control over her own body.

Macy Johns had grown furious. Andrea Kent's disappearance from the table had led the other bridesmaids, along with the bride herself, to turn all attention toward their absent friend. As maid of honor, Macy felt it was her responsibility to drag Andrea back to the table, hungover or not, so the evening's focus could remain firmly fixed on the bride and groom.

First, she had gone outside, expecting to find Andrea puking in the shrubbery. But she wasn't there. In fact, unless the bridesmaid had wandered off through the vineyard, she was no longer outside at all.

"What the hell, Andy?" Macy mumbled under her breath.

As she approached the door to get back into the venue,

she noticed another entrance, one leading to the vineyard's commercial kitchen where the caterers were likely still prepping the dessert course. The door was propped open with a chair.

'Maybe she got hungry,' Macy thought. 'She did miss the salad course and most of dinner.'

As soon as she stepped through the doorway, fear and confusion froze Macy in her tracks. The caterers, Melvin and Tamara Holmes, lay dead on the floor, blood still spreading out like some horrific Rorschach test beneath their bodies. A knife protruded from Tamara's sternum. She had been stabbed multiple times. Melvin Holmes, a vivacious and kind man known for his cheesy jokes and world-class shrimp and grits, had a portion of his head caved in by what appeared to be a cast-iron skillet.

In a room down the hall, Sara was celebrating the start of a new chapter in her life as the best man was beginning to give his speech. Macy was supposed to speak next. All of that seemed worlds away as she gazed in shock at the carnage before her. She crossed the room as far from the dead caterers as she could manage, knowing she needed to find a phone and call the police even though it would bring her sister's wedding celebration to a screeching halt.

Near the door to the hallway, hidden by a table, she found two of the servers dead, their throats slit. It occurred to Macy that the murderer could still be loose inside the venue and the safest place to be was in the ballroom with the hundred or more wedding guests. Besides, her phone was in her mother's purse. She could retrieve it and call the police from the safety of a large crowd.

Macy pushed the door open slowly and peeked down the hall. It was empty and quiet. She cautiously stepped out of the murder scene and made her way toward the event space. At the other end of the corridor, roughly eight feet from the ballroom door, she found Andrea Kent covered in abstract splatters of blood.

"Oh my god, Andy," Macy said, running toward her sister's friend. "Are you okay?"

She grabbed the bloody bridesmaid and began examining her for wounds.

"Who *did* this to you? What's happen—"

Her words were cut short by a strange feeling in her stomach. It was cold and drove all thought from her mind. She looked down to see the handle of chef's knife jutting out of her belly until Andrea pulled it free and plunged it in again. And again.

As she fell to the ground, Macy Johns tried to ask *why* this was happening. She needed to know what would cause one of the most kind and decent people she knew to do something so horrible. But when she looked up at the young woman she had known since middle school, all she could see was her smile.

It was wrong somehow. All feral teeth and depravity. Inhuman.

It was the last thing Macy Johns would ever see of a night filled with blood and consequences.

CHAPTER 11/
HUSK

Erwin Barrie was normally the picture of poise. This had led a few of his more jealous competitors to paint his serenity as boredom, both with the pursuit of the antiques he often sold at auction and with the lack of a real challenge. Acquiring rarities came easily to Erwin due in no small part to his family's stature and inexhaustible wealth. His professional reputation was sterling. His track record unblemished. He had every reason to feel calm.

Yet, on that humid summer day in New York City, Erwin Barrie felt anxious. His latest purchase had taken more than a decade to track down and attain. He had first negotiated with a private owner, then with the Sharjah Museum of Islamic Civilization in the United Arab Emirates. Finally, he had struck a bargain with a black-market dealer, who had likely procured the artifact from the thieves responsible for the heist which had recently scarred the Sharjah's reputation for security. Following several clandestine meetings and smaller transfers to a Swiss bank account, accompanied by a cash drop to a one-armed middleman known simply as The Scimitar, the *Husk of Erra* would finally take its place in Erwin Barrie's coveted collection.

One of the doormen for the Malden Towers, a young Hispanic man named Elazar, had called moments earlier to tell Erwin his prize had been delivered and the crate was on its way up to the penthouse. It was escorted by Elazar's mentor, senior doorman Carl, and the building's valet, a young African American woman named Tiara Randall.

Erwin had taken an interest in Miss Randall when he learned she was majoring in cultural anthropology. He was impressed with her curiosity almost as much as her nearly encyclopedic knowledge of Akkadian mythology and, thus, had awed her with hyperbolic tales of his quest to obtain the Husk.

Erwin did not wait for the doorbell to ring. He stood looking for Carl (whose last name he had never bothered to learn) and Tiara within the frame of his open door. When the elevator arrived with a cheerful 'ding', he watched with bated breath as they rolled the crate toward him on a utility cart typically utilized for mail delivery. The excitement in Tiara's eyes delighted him. Yet, as bright and filled with potential as she was, she barely had an inkling as to how much the acquisition meant to a collector of rarities like Erwin Barrie.

Carl and his apprentice, Elazar, had been appropriately intrigued by the various crates frequently delivered to the penthouse owner, often with considerable security measures in place. But their curiosity about this piece was trivial at best. They had no real understanding of the cultural or reputational value of claiming the *Husk of Erra,* nor of its history so rich with superstition and mystery.

"You should've seen the grim reaper who dropped this off, Mr. Barrie," Tiara said as soon as they approached his door. "You'd have thought he was one of those film noir secret agent types passing off a cache of uranium. Glad he came while it was still light out. Malden still hasn't replaced the lights along the drive after lightning struck them last month. Aside from the light under the awning, it gets pitch black out there at night."

"The seller has every reason to value security," Erwin said, stepping out of the way to let them into the penthouse. "His sales are not exactly—"

"Legal?" Carl offered, then to Tiara whispered, "The awning light is out now, too, by the by. Malden's too damn cheap to fix *anything.*"

"Let's say these sales are not encouraged by certain governments and systems of power," Erwin countered, ignoring the co-workers' gossip.

"That's what I said," Carl replied. "It ain't *legal.* Where you want this, Professor?"

Erwin Barrie had earned many degrees but was not, by any definition, a professor. Yet, throughout the 12 years Carl had been employed at Malden Towers, if he didn't refer to Erwin as "Mr. Barrie," it was as "professor." And, as Erwin couldn't be bothered to correct him daily, he had learned to let it go.

"Take it into the study," Erwin directed. "I've set a small table in there as a work surface for its unpacking. Did you remember a pry bar?"

Tiara held up the 12-inch tool which had a rubber handle not unlike the grip of a screwdriver.

"Gotcha covered, Mr. Barrie," she said excitedly. "Can't wait to get a look at this thing. Been reading up on it. Did you know that the Husk was referred to in some ancient texts as the *Tomb of Nergal*?"

Erwin smiled but, before he could speak, she continued.

"*Of course*, you did. No one knows this stuff more than you. You're Erwin Barrie, after all."

"I'm pleased you've taken an interest, Tiara. You'd be surprised at how few people your age have *any* interest in history beyond, say...the latest season of *The Bachelor*."

He followed them into the study where they carefully lifted the crate onto the small round table (an antique Erwin had purchased in Nepal) and allowed its new owner to look the delivery over. At roughly the size of a microwave oven, the crate gave the false impression that its contents were more sizeable than they were.

"Pry bar, please," Erwin asked after slipping on a pair of nitrile gloves.

Tiara handed him the tool and then took a position behind him. She wanted to see the *Husk of Erra* for herself.

"Carl," Erwin said without looking his way, "once I've removed the artifact, please dispose of the crate and its packing materials. I won't have further need of them. This piece will be staying with me."

"Whatever you say, professor," Carl said, scrolling through his cell phone.

Erwin pried the top off the box and carefully removed fistfuls of packing material until he was able to see the handle of a smaller receptacle. Gripping it, he pulled free a Pelican case that was locked shut with a minuscule padlock.

"Tiara, if you'd please go to the middle drawer of my desk, you'll find the key for this lock. It was provided for me when I made the final payment."

The young woman hurried to the desk and returned promptly with the tiny key.

"Thank you, dear. I know that neither of you are fully aware of all the trouble I've gone through to acquire this piece but let me assure you that this is the fulfillment of many years of pursuit...not to mention *great* expense. Though its history is shrouded in mystery, the Husk has been my obsession for many a year."

"I felt that way about trying to wrangle season tickets for the Yankees," Carl said. "Seemed like it'd never happen until my cousin, Louisa, married a dude that works security for the team and landed me a sweet deal."

Erwin feigned a smile and offered, "I suppose, then, you *understand* my elation."

"I get it," Carl said, brushing the packing material back into the emptied crate. "You're super stoked."

"Quit jawing, Carl, and let the man have his moment," Tiara said. "I wanna see this thing."

They watched silently as Erwin placed the key in the padlock and turned it. Once it popped free, he removed the lock altogether and set it aside. Taking a deep breath, he opened the case. A smile overtook his features as he, at last, beheld the reward for all his efforts seated securely in its custom foam insert.

"Is that it?" Carl asked. "A little clay doll?"

"It's not a doll," Tiara argued. "It's a totem of Erra."

"You mean he got the wrong one? After all this?"

"Not *error*, old man. Erra. He was the Akkadian deity of pestilence and such. It's called a 'Husk' because it's empty on the inside. The legends say it houses all the sickness and diseases that he inflicted on people throughout the millennia."

"And you brought that thing *here*? To Malden Towers?" Carl asked, putting away his phone and backing up. "Did you learn nothing from the Covid nightmare, professor? You can't go risking the other residents with that stuff."

"It's *legend*, Carl," Erwin assured him. "Nothing more than a myth. A scary story created to control the masses."

"He's right," Tiara said. "It's just a clay figure...and a rather simple one at that compared to other archaeological finds from that period. But that's what makes it so unique."

"Okay," Carl said, returning the empty crate to the mail trolley. "You two enjoy your 'unique' doll. I've got to get back down to Elazar. He can't be trusted to watch the doors on his own. Always looking at his damn phone, that kid."

"Thank you for your assistance, Carl," Erwin called after him. "There'll be a sizable tip for you come the morning."

"Thanks, professor. Congratulations on your whatever-it-is," Carl shouted back.

"Whatcha gonna do with it?" Tiara asked, peering at the Husk over his shoulder.

"As I said, it's staying with me. It will be the crowning jewel to my collection."

He carefully lifted the *Husk of Erra* from the case with his gloved hands and made his way to an ornate display cabinet in the corner of the room. Standing at least a foot taller than the man himself, the well-lit depository contained the rarest artifacts in his expansive collection, each identified by a typed, rectangular placard listing its name, region, and estimated date of origin. He had prepared a label and a space for the Husk in advance of its arrival.

"Can you please open that for me, Tiara? I'd rather keep both hands on this little darling."

"Of course," she said, scooting around him to open the case. "I'm not gonna set off alarms or booby traps or anything, am I?"

"No, no. I unlocked it and disabled the alarm when Elazar called to say you were on your way up."

She opened the case and watched as he gingerly placed the object in its new home.

"What do you think?"

"The photos I saw of it certainly didn't do it justice," the young woman admitted. "It somehow looks both delicate and like it should weigh a ton, you know?"

"It's been studied. Not with the *latest* technology, of course, but still. A scan twenty years ago was unable to determine the individual components of the clay."

"They don't know who made it either," Tiara replied. "That came up in everything I read. So many images of Erra show details like an ornate beard or him holding something in his hands. This is just a simplistic figure. Reminds me of a primitive *Matryoshka* doll."

"I can see that," he replied with a smile. "But we can't open this one up to find others, I'm afraid. As your research revealed, it is, in fact, quite hollow."

"If you don't mind me asking, Mr. Barrie, how did the *Husk of Erra* come to be your white whale?"

Erwin closed the cabinet and then, with an app on his

phone, locked it and armed the alarm.

"It's rather simple, Miss Randall. So many collectors were after it, many of them as obsessed as I have been, that I just had to beat them to the punch so to speak. To prove to myself and my competitors, I suppose, that I could get it. That there was *nothing* beyond my reach."

"You sure showed 'em, I guess. I know you said I can't tell anyone it's here…and I won't, but…*man*, it's cool to be able to actually see it up close after reading so much about it."

"The *Husk of Erra* isn't something you'd have ever heard about in a class, Tiara. You only knew to study up on it after I told you I had procured it. I'd suggest taking a lesson from that. Namely, that not everything of interest is found in a textbook. Nor in the insipid anecdotes of your professors whose only adventures have taken place within the confines of their own imaginations."

She laughed at that.

"They try to make it sound like they're Indiana Jones when they're really just—"

"History nerds with large book collections," Erwin offered with a wry smile. "I make no pretense regarding adventure, young lady. I've let my money and reputation do *most* of the work for me. You'll not find me digging up tombs in the dark or eating the brains of monkeys."

"I gotta head back down to the valet stand before Mr. Walden docks my pay," she said with a weak smile. "Thanks for letting me check it out."

"Of course, Tiara. Always happy to encourage the passion for archeology and history in others."

Erwin escorted the young woman to the door and secured its many locks after she had gone. He then returned to his office and sat at his desk, staring contentedly at his prize in the corner display case.

The resonant reverberation of a gong woke Erwin from a deep sleep at 2:38 that morning. He sat up in his bed in a cold sweat with terror charging through his heart like a thoroughbred. He took a few slow, deep breaths and calmed himself. It was surely nothing but the remnants of a dream. Though his home was filled with many unique items from numerous eras and civilizations, a gong was not among them.

"You're just too excited, old boy," he whispered to himself in the darkness of his room. "Big day. *Bigger* triumph."

He swung his legs over the edge of the bed and took another deep breath. After sliding his feet into his slippers and putting on his robe, he shuffled off to the kitchen and poured himself a finger of rye. As he sipped, he thought he heard a strange noise emanating from the office. A glance toward the front door assured him that the penthouse remained secure. Still, he took his glass and went to check it out.

The *Husk of Erra* rested safely behind the display case in

the corner of his office. Except…

Erwin stepped closer to the cabinet and peered inside. The Husk, though secure, was damaged. A small crack had formed on one of the legs of the figure and extended up its left side until it stopped just under the arm.

"No!" the collector said with a gasp, moving quickly to the hidden panel that contained a keypad from which he could disarm the alarms and unlock the cabinet. "It was *perfect* before!"

With the security system off, he opened the cabinet and then slipped on the gloves he kept in one drawer of his desk. Gently, he lifted the idol from its place and examined it. Another crack formed across its simplistic head, running midway down the back. Erwin quickly moved it to his desk where he turned on the light around the rim of the large magnifying glass he often used to closely examine his treasures. The lens was attached to his desk by an adjustable swivel arm that allowed him to move it precisely where it was most needed without having to hold it himself.

Carefully, he turned the Husk of Erra in his gloved hands, examining the cracks that continued to form on its surface.

"It's a phony," he mumbled to himself. "It *has* to be."

But it wasn't. He had done the research and verified its authenticity himself. The Husk was real…and it was crumbling in his hands.

In the shadows to his right, someone spoke in a language

familiar to Erwin Barrie yet not in a dialect he could easily place. The voice startled him, causing him to grip the *Husk of Erra* so tightly that the two larger cracks on the idol's surface spread out to meet one another, halving his treasure in his hands. His eyes quickly scanned the room for an intruder as a single bead of sweat ran down his forehead. He was still alone, it seemed, but now with two halves of an idol in the palm of one hand.

He set the remnants on his desk and cursed under his breath. It wasn't until he turned off the light of the magnifying glass that he became aware of the figure standing directly across from him. In the dark, it appeared only as a silhouette, roughly the size of a man but more feral in its posture. Erwin shrieked in surprise and turned the light back on. Whoever or *whatever* had been there a second earlier was gone.

He looked over to his empty glass of rye and shook his head.

"You're losing it, old boy. Best not to let a bad purchase rob you of your sanity."

He left the broken idol on his desk, retrieved his empty glass, and departed the office for the kitchen where he poured another drink.

"We'll just sleep it off then, shall we?" he muttered, before taking another sip of rye. "Tomorrow, we'll get to the bottom of this treachery. Starting with our rapacious one-armed middleman."

Erwin shuffled back to his bed and fell into a restless sleep brimming with nightmares.

He dreamt of the mysterious broker, The Scimitar, whom Erwin suspected might have kept the real *Husk of Erra* along with his cut of the illegal transaction. He'd likely attempt to sell the genuine artifact himself or endeavor to extort more money from Erwin. Either way, the collector didn't dislike dreaming of the man's demise. In fact, he could see it clearly in his sleeping mind where it seemed the superstitions about the Husk were somehow true and The Scimitar and his crew began to succumb to the effects of leprosy.

Had Erwin been awake with access to his conscious knowledge, he'd have laughed at the notion. Leprosy, though once a deadly threat to many populations of the ancient world, is perfectly curable with modern medicine. And it certainly didn't accelerate at the rate he imagined. In his dream, it practically ate Scimitar and his felonious friends alive, ravaging their bodies with malevolent expediency.

His dreams then turned to Elazar and Carl. Standing outside the aging Malden Towers in their matching uniforms like ragtag soldiers protecting the building's occupants from solicitors and unwanted guests, they remained a welcoming presence for every resident in need of a broad smile or a hand with unwieldy packages. Elazar was telling Carl all about his mother's *Ajiaco Cubano*, a dish he described as "chicken soup but with actual flavor." The older doorman argued that he was more of a "chili kind o' guy" seconds before he began to cough uncontrollably. Elazar, concerned for his mentor, crossed in front of the building's entrance as he, too, started to cough, expelling blood and tissue as he fell to his knees.

Erwin tossed in his bed, distressed by the horror unfolding in his dreams. Though he had little in common with the Elizars and Carls of the world, he found both men to be pleasant, helpful, and without guile. Watching them succumb to some strange pathogen was awful. A criminal like The Scimitar might deserve death for his sundry illegal exploits, but the kind doormen who, without fail, greeted Erwin daily with a smile? *Never.* Still, he was trapped with them in the nightmare, watching as they fell to their knees and then to their faces, as dead as the ancient Babylonians who had once offered sacrifices to Erra.

Erwin awoke screaming. In the other room, someone was feverishly knocking on his penthouse door. The clock read 8:43 a.m. He stared at it and rubbed his eyes. He hadn't slept past 8 a.m. in nearly 20 years. His internal clock simply didn't allow it.

'I guess that second sip of rye was uncalled-for,' he thought.

The knocking continued, a frantic rhythm.

"I'm coming, damn it!" he shouted, rubbing his aching head. "Cease your pounding!"

Upon opening his front door, Erwin was confronted with dread personified in the young frame of Tiara Randall, whose eyes were red and swollen with tears. Her apparent confusion and desperation prompted a response within Erwin that he had never realized he was capable of: fatherly concern.

"Dear me, girl, what's the matter?"

"It's Carl and Elazar," she said, pushing past him into the penthouse. "They're dead."

He froze in place and swallowed the lump he suddenly found in his throat.

"What?"

Erwin escorted the girl to the sofa and prompted her to sit. He sat beside her and placed a gentle hand on her shoulder.

"I found them," she said, her voice shaking with emotion. "I took the early shift today because I have a date tonight. Police think the two of them were lying there dead all night. Mr. Malden never had the damn light fixed under the awning. Who knows how many people drove by and never saw them? They were both off the clock at 11 p.m., so it had to have happened before then."

Erwin's thoughts were filled with questions, but one rose to the surface and past his lips.

"Did the police say *how* they died?"

Tiara shook her head.

"Just that they looked really sick. The cops are downstairs now with someone from the CDC having building security give them access to the cameras. I heard one of them say they hoped it wasn't contagious."

"Strange," Erwin said, recalling his dream.

"Not strange," Tiara argued. "You brought the Husk here, Mr. Barrie. Then this happens? That can't be coincidence."

"Of course it can. The legends around the Husk are just silly superstitions. You said so yourself."

"That was *before* my co-workers, one of whom was my age and healthy as an ox, keeled over dead from a strange medical condition, Mr. Barrie."

"Carl never *touched* the Husk, Tiara. And poor Elazar never even got a look at it. How would the idol have done them harm, exactly? Hell, girl, *you* were closer to it than either of them and you seem just fine aside from your grief."

Tiara nodded but remained unconvinced.

"Look, Tiara, no one is more upset than I am about Carl and young Elazar. Whatever happened to them certainly took them too soon. But blaming the supernatural for their deaths won't solve anything. If they had something that could be passed to others, I'm sure the police will evacuate us all for our own safety. Until such time, it's best not to speculate."

Part of him wanted to tell the girl the Husk was a fake, that it had fallen apart in his hands, but he feared it might add to her anxiety and push her toward shock or, worse still, madness.

"I blame myself for these worries you have, dear girl. I should never have told you about my pursuit of the Husk. If you hadn't researched the lore, you wouldn't be so afraid of monsters in the dark. I assure you, child, that whatever ended the lives of those poor gentlemen was of this earth not the spirit."

"You don't believe in the supernatural?" she asked. "That there's more to reality than our senses can detect?"

"I've studied ancient cultures throughout my many years. I've never seen any evidence of such things…only blind belief and ancient narratives used to maintain power and control. Erra wasn't *real*, child. He was nothing more than an invention of men desperate to explain the plagues and sicknesses that swept the world in those times."

"You're *sure?*"

"I am. Will you be alright? Can I call someone to take you home?"

Tiara shook her head.

"Everyone in the building has to stay put until the police question the staff and all the residents. They're trying to make sure no one saw anything out of the ordinary."

"I see."

"I'll just wait downstairs in the lobby until they're done with me."

"Nonsense. You can stay right *here*. Let me make you a cup of coffee. Or would you prefer tea?"

"Coffee is fine," she said, managing a half smile. "Thank you."

"No need for thanks," he replied, standing and making his way toward the kitchen. "We're all in this together until the police have their answers."

As he went through the motions of making coffee, Erwin's mind raced. The doormen had died just as they had in his dreams. The notion seemed impossible but, given what Tiara Randall had described, he couldn't deny it.

Except, of course, he *had* denied it. He couldn't tell Tiara, or anyone else for that matter, about his dreams. Who would believe him? And, if they did, they'd want to take the Husk…or, at the very least, investigate his procurement of it. On the off chance it was proven a fake, he had still purchased it illegally with full knowledge that it was stolen. *No.* Better to let the police come to their own conclusions. One coincidence was not reason enough to sacrifice all his hard work.

"How do you take your coffee, Tiara?" Erwin called from the kitchen. "Cream and sugar?"

The girl on his sofa didn't answer.

"Miss Randall?"

He stepped back into the living room to discover the girl

was no longer present. Erwin knew instantly where she had gone. The office. He found her standing with her back to the door, staring at the broken pieces of the *Husk of Erra* still laying on his desk.

"What did you *do?*" the girl whispered as if all the breath had gone out of her lungs.

"It's a fake," he said, though he wasn't convinced it was true. "It began cracking last night in the case. When I pulled it out to see if I could mitigate the damage, it split in two."

"It isn't fake. Don't you see, Mr. Barrie? It killed them. It's killing *us.*"

"Don't be so dramatic, child. We're fine."

"Are we?"

She turned to confront him, and he recoiled in horror. Her once pretty young face was now covered in pustules of fiery crimson, oozing and dripping to her valet uniform. She raised a hand and pointed it his way. It, too, was ruined by the affliction.

"You killed me, Mr. Barrie! *You* did this!"

"Let me call someone, Tiara. The paramedics may still be downstairs!"

But it was too late. Tiara Randall, as sharp as a tack and destined for greatness, collapsed gasping for air at his feet. Her final breath came mere seconds later.

"No, no!" Erwin cried, kneeling to check her pulse. "Not

this! Come on, Tiara!"

But she was dead. As were poor Carl and young Elazar. And in that moment, Erwin Barrie, cynical collector of things, knew in his heart that The Scimitar was dead, too… along with his men. All because Erwin brought the *Husk of Erra* into their paths.

He stood to his feet and stared at the remnants of the idol atop his desk. He knew in the depths of him that he would be next.

But Erwin Barrie refused to be a victim…not to some ancient Akkadian deity. If he was fated to die, it would be on *his* terms and his alone. He ran to the balcony doors and threw them open. From 24 stories up, death upon impact would be instantaneous. The fall itself, a frightening hell that he had more than earned.

A sudden weakness overtook him. Not fear, but something toxic and deadly coursing through his body, racing him to the finish. He jumped over the railing while he still had the strength to move. As the ground rushed up to meet him, Erwin felt himself withering from the inside. When he struck the pavement, his body broke apart like an empty piñata, a mere husk of the man he had once been.

Wilhelm Salles moved through the penthouse with great purpose. Around him, his staff worked to catalog and secure the many antiques, treasures, and artifacts that had once belonged to his competitor, Erwin Barrie. It had been three months since tragedy had swept through the Malden Towers, ending four lives in less than 12 hours. At first, officials had suspected an outbreak of some kind. Those inclined to conspiracy theories wondered if it had been a biological attack…a test run for something larger. The investigation turned up nothing solid and, as Erwin Barrie had no heirs, the penthouse and its contents had been auctioned to the highest bidder, namely Wilhelm.

While his staff worked throughout the rest of the residence, the infamous collector focused his attention on the office. Even the books lining the bookshelves were rarities and first printings worth a small fortune. But the treasure that had *immediately* drawn his eye sat in an ornate and well-secured cabinet in one corner of the room. Each item within it had been labeled with care. These were clearly his former competitor's most prized acquisitions. Many, he assumed, had been purchased illegally. Not that Wilhelm could cast judgement. He'd been known to purchase a few hard to acquire pieces from less-than-legitimate sources himself.

He scanned each shelf, writing down the names of the items in his memo pad. On the third, he paused and leaned closer to the case to get a better look.

"The *Husk of Erra*," he whispered in awe. "Erwin, you old *devil*. How the hell did you get your hands on this?"

The piece was remarkably old and in flawless condition.

Legend held that it was hollow, a husk to be worshipped in place of the god, Erra, the Akkadian deity of disease and pestilence.

Wilhelm smirked. He couldn't imagine anyone had ever believed such *nonsense*.

CHAPTER 12/
THE POISON PEN: THE CURSE

G. Dalton Lumley had made a name for himself writing horror tales and gripping thrillers. For more than 20 years, he'd been exactly what most authors only hoped to be: *successful*. As he investigated each news link sent by his agent and friend, Carol Breen, however, the author worried those days might be over.

Somehow, while writing a new series of short horror tales, Lumley had inadvertently yet accurately predicted several gruesome events before they happened. To his agent and her contact at Lôr (a publisher they hoped to secure a contract with) it appeared that the writer was merely using the news cycle as a source of inspiration. That was problematic because it suggested Lumley had run out of his own ideas while also seeming insensitive to the victims of real tragedies. The author worried it could also make him a suspect in those crimes.

"You can relax on that front, Gentry," Carol assured him over the phone. "Nobody in their right mind is gonna publish this stuff. And that Giamatti fella at Lôr has enough trouble on his plate now that he can't bring you into their fold. I doubt he's looking to tie you up with police inquiries. Besides, you'd need to be Harry Houdini to get to all those places in time to commit the crimes and we all know you've practically been a hermit since *A Fog of Fear* flopped out of the gate."

"You're *so* kind," Gentry sighed.

"I'm a realist, old friend. Stop fretting about those articles and wrap your noodle around a new story. A bestseller can cover a multitude of sins, you know. That said, if you pull crap like this again, friend or not, you're gonna be looking for a new agent."

"Carol, I know you don't believe me, but…I didn't do *anything* but write a dozen or so new stories. I would never do the sort of thing you believe I did, and it irks me to know you think I would."

"So how do you explain it, Gentry?"

"I-I can't."

"Then all we have is what it looks like. Unless you think you're writing with magic genie ink or something, the only explanation is that you cribbed your ideas straight from the news."

"Aside from the Mathers murder out in California, I wrote all of those stories *before* the events were reported. Come on, Carol! You can't seriously believe I can predict the future… even if it's only a day or two in advance."

"Look, whatever the truth is, the results are the same and we've got to deal with them. So, let's focus on that."

"Fine," Gentry said through clenched teeth. "I'll write something fresh tonight. But if it becomes a news story tomorrow, I might lose my godforsaken mind."

"Your career, too, Gentry. And don't forget it."

With that final remark, she hung up, leaving the author to sit alone with his frustrations until Amanda entered with a pimento cheese and bacon sandwich and a cold glass of sweet tea.

"I was standing outside for a minute," she confessed. "It sounded a bit intense in here."

"She thinks I'm trying to pull something," Gentry replied. "She doesn't *want* to, I know, but there's no logical explanation for why this is happening. Every story I've written since I got back on the horse is somehow connected to real events that happen within a day or two of me writing about them. But, Amanda, I've written these stories like I've written everything I've ever put my name on…using nothing but my own imagination."

"You did say they just *came* to you. Could you have…I don't know, tapped into something?"

"How? Psychically? I don't believe in psychics and fortune-tellers, Amanda. And that woman in California who murdered her husband? She claimed 'The Eyes' killed him."

"And 'The Eyes' were in *your* story," Amanda reminded.

"Yes but, in *my* story, the killer was a demonic entity," Gentry said. "The threat was supernatural, not something real. So, unless you believe her husband really was killed by a demon—"

"But, Gent, don't you believe that there is more to this world…t-to reality than what the five senses can grasp?"

"No," Gentry said flatly. "No, I don't. And given that my career may go the way of the Dodo, Amanda, I'd rather not bring the fantastical into it. The facts are hard enough to believe without adding speculation into the mix."

"What about the pen?"

"What *about* the pen?"

"What if it's cursed or something?"

"What did I just say? I don't believe in curses. Even if I did, why would anyone curse a fountain pen?"

"I don't know. Why would anyone curse anything? I didn't say I *understood* it. I'm just throwing things out there."

"I love my new fountain pen, dear," he said, offering her a weak smile. "It might be the kindest gift I've ever received. But I feel fairly confident in saying that you didn't give me a cursed pen."

"I don't know," she replied with a wink. "I got one *hell* of a deal on it."

"Out. *Out* of my office," he said, shaking his head. "Save your dad jokes for your next girls night out. I have to try and salvage my career."

Long after Amanda had gone and Gentry had taken a few bites of his sandwich while staring into the abyss of a blank page, he remembered Carol Breen's comment about "magic genie ink" followed by Amanda's suggestion of a cursed pen. He rubbed at his temples, cracked his neck, and then looked at the blank page again.

"No harm in testing their theories, I suppose," he mumbled to himself.

He took the fountain pen and, across the top of the page, wrote:

Michael Giamatti is desperate to sign G. Dalton Lumley. He's willing to overlook a series of what must surely be coincidences.

He then pulled the bottle of ink from his drawer and searched for a suitable writing instrument. In a box near the bottom of his filing cabinet, he found a glass dip pen, a gift given to him long ago by an artist friend. He hadn't enjoyed writing with it, but it had seemed rude to regift it. Thus, it sat unused until Gentry found a sudden need to prove to himself the supernatural did not, in fact, exist.

Mumbling beneath his breath about the insanity of the

moment, he dipped the swirled nib of the glass pen into ink and scrawled near the bottom of the page:

Carol Breen had a change of heart. She believes deep down that Gentry would never make her look fool-ish. Feeling bad about their last conversation, she picks up the phone to call him and apologize.

He sat back and shook his head before crumbling up the paper and tossing it into the waste bin.

'You're losing it, Gentry,' he thought. 'Just write a damn story.'

And write he did.

He wrote a story about a bridesmaid whose missing memory of the night before spells trouble not only for herself but for the entire wedding party. He followed it up with the tale he had mentioned to Amanda the night before: the story of a cannibalistic dinner party. By the time he was finished with it, the evening had passed, and Amanda, already dressed in her gown, had come to check on him.

"I'm exhausted," he admitted. "I'll follow you up. Maybe a solid night's sleep will give way to a better day."

"I can take your mind off things," Amanda offered, "but it seems like sleep would prove more…restorative."

He chuckled at that and squeezed her tightly.

"I'm sorry I was a grump earlier," he said, kissing her soft-ly. "I'll try to do better tomorrow."

The next morning, after a restless night of fretting over the strange events of the previous few days, Gentry stood in the steaming shower much longer than usual and was slow to dress and head downstairs for his obligatory cup of java. He was surprised when he didn't find Amanda in her usual perch in the kitchen. Most mornings, she sat in the window seat and watched whatever birds were taking advantage of the feeder she had installed a few springs prior.

"Amanda?"

"In your office, darling."

Gentry knew his wife nearly as well as she knew herself. Amanda's tone of voice could disclose almost anything he wanted to know about her state of mind. The inflection of those four simple words, muffled as they were from behind the closed door to his study, revealed her apprehension.

He pushed the door to the office open to find her seated at his desk. In her left hand, she held the handwritten pages he had written the night before. Her right was using the touchpad on his laptop to scan a web page.

"You read the new stories," he said, dropping into the overstuffed wing chair opposite from his desk.

"I did."

"And you *found* something? In the news, I mean."

"I believe so," she said, looking up to meet his gaze. "I found a newspaper in—"

Amanda's thought was interrupted by the ringing of Gentry's cell phone. He had forgotten to take it upstairs with him the night before. It's ringtone (an 8-bit version of Elliott Smith's "Needle in the Hay") was the one Gentry had assigned for unknown numbers.

Amanda handed the phone to her husband and leaned across his desk, curious. Not many had Gentry's private number and those who did tended to be people he had listed in his phone's directory of contacts.

"Put it on speaker," she prompted.

He did as he was asked.

"G. Dalton Lumley," he answered.

"Mr. Lumley," a man replied, "this is Michael Giamatti. I spoke with your wife the other day."

"And my agent, I believe," Gentry added, his tone a bit sourer than he intended.

"Yes, sir. I *tried* speaking to your agent this morning, but she didn't return my call and I wanted to speak with you as soon as possible. I hope you don't mind me calling."

"That will depend largely on what you *say*, Mr. Giamatti," Gentry said, prompting a stern look from Amanda.

Giamatti chuckled uncomfortably on the other end of the line.

"I'm sure you know that we had a few concerns about the

content she sent to us," Giamatti said, "though the writing itself was exactly the sort of we were looking for."

"Were," Gentry repeated.

"*Are,* Mr. Lumley. I've had a day or two to talk things over with my team and we believe that, with a tweak or two in the editing process, we can add you to the Lôr roster with minimal concern."

"Mr. Giamatti, I don't mean to be rude, so please don't take my forthrightness for disrespect. But I want to make it *abundantly* clear that every story you've seen of mine was written by me, alone, without any current news stories as a point of reference."

"Which is why our stance has softened," Giamatti said. "We *believe* you. We had a trusted source check the metadata of the files we were sent, and it was clear you forwarded those pages to Ms. Breen before the similar news stories were even reported…the exception, of course, being the Corrine Mathers story. Changes will still need to be made, of course, to distance your tales a bit from the actual events, but we no longer believe you were cannibalizing news articles for your inspiration."

"Imagine my relief," Gentry replied through clenched teeth.

"You are rightly upset with us, Mr. Lumley, but surely you understand our delicate position."

"I suppose."

"As I said, we were attempting to call Ms. Breen to let her know that we would still *very much* like for you to join us at Lôr. If you're interested, we can send Ms. Breen a contract for you to look over. I know it's likely been a stressful week, Mr. Lumley, so take whatever time you need. Just know that we would be thrilled to have you onboard."

Gentry glanced over at Amanda but found her expression difficult to read.

"Forward the contract, Mr. Giamatti, but I make no promises. I've been in this business a long, *long* time. I'm unaccustomed to accusations of cribbing my ideas."

"I believe you'll find out offer *quite* generous. Look it over. Discuss things with your agent, you wife, and your attorneys. And, again, I apologize for doubting you, Mr. Lumley, but I'm certain you understand how careful Lôr must be with such things. We live in a rather litigious society."

"Carol Breen or I will get back to you. Good day, Mr. Giamatti."

"Goodbye, Mr. Lumley."

Gentry hung up, then looked over at Amanda and asked, "What do you make of *that?*"

"I honestly don't know, Gent. I mean, just yesterday—"

"Yeah," he said, standing and walking over to the wastebasket.

Amanda watched as he retrieved a crumpled piece of paper and approached her side of the desk.

"What's that?"

"I put your theory to the test last night," he said, starting to unwrap and straighten the paper.

"What theory?"

"Well, not just yours. Carol's, too. She thought it was the ink. You thought it was the pen."

"Oh," she said, suddenly realizing what he was getting at. "What did you do?"

"See for yourself," he said, handing her the paper.

As she read it, her eyes grew ever wider until she turned to her husband, unable to speak.

"It's getting harder to believe it's a coincidence," he admitted. "I wrote that Lôr would want me anyway and—"

"And they do. But you didn't hear from Carol?"

"No."

"So, it isn't the *ink*."

"Doesn't seem so."

She stood so that she was face to face with him, fear causing her eyes to dart back and forth, searching his for answers.

"I was mostly joking when I said that," she offered. "I don't believe in curses. Not *really,* anyway. I just know that sometimes things happen that seem to be beyond what my brain can handle. I never thought…I mean, how can a pen be cursed?"

Gentry shrugged.

"Maybe we're collectively losing our minds, Amanda. Maybe there's lead in the water or…black mold somewhere we haven't seen."

"I'd almost prefer it."

"We were interrupted by the call before you told me what you found," he reminded. "Your tone and expression suggested it was *no bueno*."

"Nothing on the cannibal dinner party in Montana, thankfully, but a young woman apparently murdered several people at a wedding reception before a SWAT team took her down."

"And the details matched?"

"Like you were an eye-witness."

"What in God's name is happening?"

"I doubt God has anything to do with it," Amanda said softly. "It's likely the other guy."

"I don't believe in *any* of that."

"I'm not sure your belief matters much, Gent. This stuff is happening. It's really, truly happening."

"No one will believe it," he said, picking up the fountain pen. "No one."

"I don't believe it, either. I just…know it."

"We need another test," Gent said, slipping past her and dropping into his office chair. "Something safe. I mean, I wrote about Giamatti. No one got hurt. If everything I write comes true, what couldn't we do?"

"But what you've already done…darling, I know it wasn't intentional, but people have died."

Gentry pulled a sheet of paper from his drawer and let the nib hover over it while he thought of what to jot down.

"Maybe we shouldn't tempt fate by writing anything else," Amanda added.

But Gentry had already started writing. He wrote three simple sentences, then handed the paper to Amanda, who read them aloud.

"Carol Breen apologizes to G. Dalton Lumley for not believing in him," she read. "A pizza delivery man arrives at the residence of Amanda Lumley with a pie she never ordered. The novel *A Fog of Fear* is at the center of a bidding war for film rights."

"If I'm gonna make things happen," Gentry said, "I want it to be only good things from now on."

The doorbell rang, startling them both.

"Your pizza is here," Gentry whispered.

"It's not even 9 a.m., Gent. Nobody is delivering me a breakfast pizza, cursed pen or no."

He followed his wife to the front door. She opened it to find Carol Breen standing on their doormat, stomping out a cigarette butt with a strange look on her face.

"I'm no good at eating crow," she grumbled, not bothering to make eye contact. "But Lôr seems to want you onboard, Gentry, and they made me feel like quite the ass for not believing you. I'm sorry, pal. I just couldn't wrap my head around what was happening."

"We still can't," Amanda admitted.

"Come on it," Gentry added, offering her a smile. "Have a cup of coffee."

"We're expecting pizza for lunch."

Carol Breen wasn't sure why either of them found Amanda's comment funny, but she didn't ask any questions.

A manda was clearing away breakfast dishes when Carol excused herself from the table to answer a call on the back porch where she was free to smoke. Gentry retreated to his office where he looked over the news story Amanda had dug up about the wedding reception murders.

The photo of Andrea Kent was taken from a college sorority's web page. With her kind eyes and vibrant smile, she looked like the furthest thing from a mass murderer. According to the stories, she had been shot multiple times by the SWAT team after killing twelve people.

"I did that," Gentry whispered to himself. "She's dead because of me. All those people are dead because of me."

"You're not gonna believe this, pal," Carol said, bursting into the office without knocking. "I just got off the phone with my secretary. He's received no less than three calls from different production houses wanting to talk about the rights to that shitty London novel of yours. Today seems to be breaking your way, Gentry. Maybe you'll win the lottery next, huh?"

When he didn't respond, Carol snapped her fingers directly in front of his face.

"Earth to Gentry! You still with us?"

"Can we look over the contract tomorrow?" he asked, rubbing at his eyes with the palms of his hands. "I'm not sure I'm mentally equipped at the moment."

"Whatever floats your boat, pal. I've got film rights to negotiate now. I'm gonna head on back to the office. Walk me out?"

He did as she asked, not processing her words as she encouraged him to take a few days away from writing to clear his head. When he opened the front door to let her out, there was a teen standing on the porch, holding a pizza box, his fist up and prepared to knock.

"I've, uh, got an order for an Amanda Lumley," the boy said.

"I thought you were kidding about ordering a pizza," Carol said. "You'll have to eat it without me though, because I'm out."

Gentry fished his wallet out, paid the delivery boy, then took the pizza inside and dropped it on the kitchen counter, startling Amanda. When she saw the box, she was slack jawed.

"Oh, Gentry."

"I know."

Neither of them ate the pizza. Neither ate *anything* for the rest of the day. By the time Amanda fell asleep on the sofa in their spacious great room, Gentry had made his decision. He built a fire in the limestone fireplace and, once it was blazing hot, tossed the fountain pen into the flames. He watched as it ignited and the lacquer melted before his eyes. The nib dropped down among the embers. The ink sputtered and spattered as it boiled, leaving a few green-black blots on the white stones. Gentry wondered if his career, too, had perished in that same fire.

As he walked past the sectional, he unfolded an afghan and covered Amanda. She was sleeping peacefully. He watched the gentle rise and fall of her chest, hoping she was dreaming lovely dreams somewhere far away from the confusion of the day.

He returned to his office and powered on his laptop. He created a new document, determined to write something fresh. Something as good as *anything* he had written with that damned pen.

The blinking cursor mocked him, but Gentry didn't care. He was a writer. And whatever worlds he created digitally would never be anything but fiction.

He caught himself yawning and shook his head in defiance. Lôr wanted new Lumley novels. Hollywood was actively fighting for his film rights.

"You can *do* this," he mumbled to himself.

G entry awoke in the middle of the night, frustrated to find the empty document still staring back at him. A glance at his watch confirmed he'd been asleep for several hours. He thought for the briefest of moments about seeing if Amanda was still resting in the great room and walking them both upstairs to bed, but then he caught a glimpse of something impossible in the corner of his eye. To his right, set proudly atop a stack of paper, was the poison pen. Pristine, unharmed, and without the slightest scent of smoke.

He picked it up and snapped it in two, its green-black ink dripping through his fingers to the parquet floor beneath his desk. He stormed out of his office and to the kitchen where he threw the two halves of the pen into the trash compactor. He closed it and hit the start button, listening as the device compressed its sundry contents into a small cube. Once it was finished, he opened the compactor to make sure the cursed object was suitably destroyed.

The fountain pen was no longer in the machine.

"Honey?" yawned Amanda from the doorway. "What's with all the racket?"

He ignored his wife's question, walking past her to return to his office.

The cursed contraption awaited him at his desk.

"I've tried twice now to destroy the pen," he told her, almost afraid to go any nearer to the writing instrument. "It's always right there when I get back."

"That's not possible, is it?"

"None of this is. Yet here we are."

"What do we do?"

"I'm not sure," he admitted, "but I'll think of something."

"I wish I hadn't bought it for you," she replied, wrapping her arms around him. "I've put us in this pickle."

"You didn't make me write such horrors," he said, kissing her forehead. "That was me. My *imagination* cost those people their lives."

"You couldn't have known, darling."

"I know *now*. And it's going to stop. Go on up to bed, Amanda. I'll figure something out."

"Maybe you could just lock it away. Put it in the safe and never touch it again."

"I think it *wants* me to write a story," Gentry said, rubbing at the stubble on his chin. "I stared at a blank page so long I fell asleep. I don't think I'll ever be able to tell another story until I'm rid of the thing. It's made me dependent on it."

"Nonsense. You were a gifted writer long before I bought the damned thing."

"*Were*," he repeated. "That's past tense, dear. You know it and I know it. And I won't be tempted by that demonic, broad-nibbed bringer of chaos. It's got to go. I'll find a way."

She hesitated to leave him, but Gentry finally convinced her to head to bed without him. Alone, in his office, he pondered the pen. He thought of the merchant Amanda had purchased it from and wondered if he, too, had sought to free himself of the burden of its power by selling the fountain pen to a well-meaning stranger. How many had died before the pen had even come to the frustrated author?

"Mightier than the sword, indeed," he mumbled softly, turning the pen in his hand. "You've certainly spilled more than your share of blood. And I'll not have you killing anyone else on my account."

Seated at his desk, he pulled a clean sheet of paper from his drawer.

"You've done good when I've written it so," Gentry whispered. "Let's see if that solves the problem."

At the top of the page, he wrote a simple sentence:

G. Dalton Lumley no longer controls the cursed fountain pen.

He wondered if more specificity was in order, but writers were taught to keep it simple, to write only the words necessary to convey the idea. There was no need to use thirty if five would do. Gentry stared at the sentence for a moment before deciding it was acceptable. He would test it, of course, but in the morning…after a few solid hours of much-needed sleep. He'd write something simple and see if the curse had, in fact, been broken. But surely it had been. It made whatever he wrote a reality. Why would this be any different?

He was halfway up the stairs, bound for bed, when he heard glass shatter.

It sounded like it came from the kitchen, so he turned and walked back downstairs, half-expecting to find Amanda cleaning up whatever mess she'd made while on the hunt for something to satisfy her sweet tooth.

Instead of his wife, he found two masked men, one of whom brandished a pistol. Before he could process the strange situation, the shorter of the two robbers spotted Gentry and, in his surprise, fired his weapon. The stunned writer hit the floor hard, feeling every millimeter of the hole that had just been punched through his chest.

At the sound of the gunshot, Amanda screamed from

somewhere upstairs, and the man with the gun ran up after her. A moment later, a second shot rang out and any hope Gentry had that Amanda would survive the encounter perished with her. He remained teetering on the edge of consciousness as they ransacked the house, taking anything of value.

The timetable for the robbery had clearly been impacted by the sudden need for violence. The thieves-turned-gunmen were fast but sloppy, missing art pieces of great value in their rush to take electronics. They argued about the safe in the office. One of them, a tall and slender sort with a bit of a lisp, swore he could get into it before the cops arrived. The other, the man in charge who had shot Gentry and Amanda Lumley, assured him it wasn't worth it. They'd settle for the electronics and the silver they had nicked from the butler's pantry.

As he lay there dying and mourning the loss of his beloved, Gentry knew death had come to him because of the pen. In his desperation to be rid of it, he had given up control of the cursed object and made someone else its master. Or, worse still, had freed the pen of any need for one.

"Put that down," the head thief said from somewhere in the office. "No one writes with that shit anymore."

"You think I don't know that?" the slender crook said. "That's because it's antique. Probably worth a small fortune if I knew someone who sold this kind of junk."

"Well, you don't. So put it back and let's get the hell out

of here."

"Maybe I'll keep it for myself, then," the thin criminal said. "This fella was some big-time book writer, yeah? Might make me seem distinguished and shit."

"Yeah, right. Get you a monocle, too. That'll get your ass beaten *real* good."

"Shut up, man! I'm taking it. You took the watch."

"I can *sell* the watch."

They reentered the kitchen, passing by Gentry as if he was nothing more than a rug.

"Don't take it," he struggled. "The pen…it's—"

A swift kick from the leader of the masked men robbed Gentry of his final breath. As his vision grew dark, he heard the skinny one say:

"See, I told you that pen had to be worth something. You see how afraid he was that we were taking it?"

"That doesn't mean anything. He was already half dead."

"Still," the thief replied, "I'm keeping it."

CHAPTER 13/
THE EYES OF THE MARGRAVE

The gate guards at the Lancaster State Psychiatric Hospital were too preoccupied with a Dodgers game to notice the incredibly fast and agile figure leaping over the 15-foot wall and landing on the opposte side with feline grace. Likewise, the orderlies on the third floor, distracted as they were by their shift manager's tales of a wild Vegas getaway, missed the figure slinking through the lightless hallways. The silent infiltrator may as well have been a ghost.

The prisoner appeared to be sleeping soundly when the intruder entered his locked room, snuck past the cell's other occupant, and knelt beside his cot.

"Evan," the warrior whispered, ignoring the strange tingle at the base of his spine. "Wake up. I've come for you."

Convicted murderer, Evan Richmond, sat up and blinked at the stranger groggily.

"W-who are you?"

"We haven't met. I am called Darke, and I—"

"You! You were the one in my apartment that night…

fighting with that *thing* that killed my friends."

"You are correct. I *was* there that night. I had been called to your aid by my apprentice, Dylan."

Evan's eyes narrowed in the dark, taking in the sight of his would-be savior. The stranger looked like something out of a dystopian novel, bare-chested and tattooed with a ragged cape held around his neck by a frayed cord. Each of his forearms bore a vambrace, though the one on the stranger's left arm seemed to be technological in nature whereas the one on the right seemed to just be strips of leather wound from elbow to wrist.

"Dylan was here," Evan told the man, casting a glance to his roommate's bunk and lowering his voice to a whisper. "A few months after I arrived here, he appeared in my room, just as you have now. He said he wasn't sure he could prove my innocence but he would try. And, if he could, he would come back and get me out of here. You, uh, look a lot like him, you know."

"So I'm told. What else did Dylan say?" Darke asked, sniffing the air. Something was setting him on edge, but he couldn't put his finger on the cause of his concern.

"Only that he was looking for *you*. He said someone had prevented him from arriving to help me. Even the phone calls he made came through as a garbled mess that night. But he did say you were the one I had seen fighting those…um, 'Eyes' that killed my friends."

"Believe me when I say the horror you faced that night will trouble you no more."

"Well, that Dylan guy was asking me a bunch of questions. He said that he'd been looking for you everywhere but couldn't find any trace of you. He thought maybe the necromancer had killed you…or you'd killed each other."

"That's odd. I returned to our…um, base of operations immediately after my foe was vanquished to find Dylan had answered a call for *my* aid." Darke took a deep breath and considered the prisoners words, comparing and contrasting them to what little he had been able to ascertain himself. "He never returned. My instincts lead me to believe whoever interfered with his attempt to save your friends may have also set a trap for my young friend."

"Well, he isn't *here*," Evan said, dropping back onto his cot. "I haven't seen hide nor hair of the guy since he swore he'd come back for me. I guess that promise was DOA, and I was just too stupid to get it."

"While it's true that I came here looking for Dylan, I *also* came for you, Evan. In Dylan's absence, his vows are mine to keep."

Evan shot upright in the bed and swung his legs over the side.

"Don't play games with my emotions, Cosplay Guy. Are you or are you *not* busting me out of here?"

"It isn't that simple, I'm afraid."

Evan's hopeful expression soured into skepticism.

"It never is, is it?" he asked. "Explain it to me slowly…like I'm not a wannabe superhero from Magicland."

"The being who killed your friends should never have existed in *this* reality. The supernatural, apart from the creative workings of the Author of all things, was not written into its foundations."

"Your boy said as much. Not that I understood half of what *he* said, either. You guys just love speaking in riddles, don't you?"

"It would require tremendous power, the likes of which I have never encountered, to even connect to a reality outside one's own, let alone transport such a threat across the connection. Whoever is behind all this used their access to unleash chaos across several narratives…yours included."

"You're saying someone just dropped a monster into my world for fun?"

"More likely it was meant as a distraction…or perhaps a lure to draw me or my protégé to a specific place and time within this narrative," Darke said. "As I researched the origin of this incursion, I uncovered that the trouble began with a fountain pen which—"

"A pen? Are you shitting me?"

"A pen with the power of sub-creation."

"Like any *other* pen."

"Quite the contrary. If you were to pick up an average ball-point and write a story, you would indeed become a sub-creator, Evan, but that creation would manifest purely within a reality of its own. The writing instrument I'm speaking of, however, contains the power to manifest whatever is written with it into *this* world…often with horrific results."

"You're saying someone wrote the boogey-man into being and it led to me being imprisoned in a nut house for a crime I didn't commit?"

Darke looked down at his left vambrace. Its interface, Poe, offered nothing but general information about the timeline and the psychiatric hospital currently acting as Evan Richmond's prison.

"Strange," he said softly.

"Strange isn't the word for it," Evan replied. "Do you have any idea how long I've been mentally unraveling in this hellhole?"

"No. Which is quite unusual. Your story, Evan, was reasonably clear before Dylan was sent to intervene on your behalf. After you encountered 'The Eyes,' however, your story—"

"What?"

Darke took a deep breath and considered what he was about to reveal. He studied Evan's eyes a moment and then proceeded.

"When I researched your childhood, I found a pattern I know quite well. It is, in fact, why I believe you were targeted...though I cannot prove it."

"Do tell, Sherlock."

"Had your trajectory not been changed at different points along your timeline...including the attempt on your life and the murder of your friends, I have every reason to believe you could have been called to serve the greater narrative, much like myself and young Dylan."

"Forgive me if I don't find *that* tidbit comforting. You two haven't exactly been heroes in my book."

"I understand your frustration, even though our intentions were noble."

"You're saying a monster was thrown into the mix and *now* what? What's my...what'd you call it? *Trajectory?* What's my trajectory now?"

Darke's eyes narrowed.

"I found nothing *else* about your story. It's like nothing else was written after Dylan's visit with you. And that simply cannot be."

"I don't pretend to understand you any better than I did the kid," Evan said. "All I care about...all I've *ever* cared about...is getting out of this place. Now, can you do that or not?"

"I can. My point was only that I will need to place you

somewhere where I can still keep tabs on you…in case the threat to your life was not ended when I destroyed the necromancer."

"Then I hope you have a plan, buddy, because I'm no ninja…or whatever you're supposed to be in that getup. I've kept in shape, but I'm not exactly capable of parkouring my way out of here. If I was, I wouldn't need your help."

"It's as simple as opening a door," Darke assured him. "I only came in the hard way to get a good look at their security layout in the off chance we ran into trouble."

"Then what are we waiting for?"

The warrior stood and walked to the door, placing his ear to it.

"This way," he said.

"Hold up," Evan replied. "Where are we going? I mean, anywhere but here is great, but I'd like to have some idea of what to expect."

"I have a new identity for you, complete with all the necessary papers. You'll be free to start over."

"Start over *where?*"

"A small town in Iowa. From there, anywhere you like."

"Okay, then. Let's do this."

Darke studied Evan. Something about him was off.

He glanced back down at his left vambrace, hoping its

artificial intelligence, Poe, would have something helpful to tell him. Throughout his tenure as an agent of the Great Library, she had been his constant companion and guide when crossing from his home between worlds into the story where he was needed. Her knowledge of the ever-expanding Evermore was second only to the Author Himself.

Though Poe had both a voice and persona of her own, she had stopped speaking to Darke some time ago, relaying information via the digital interface on his arm instead. She was still as useful as she had always been, but he missed talking to her. The work he did was often lonely and friends were not easy to come by. Along with Ed the Raven and his protege, Dylan, she had been his only family for some time.

Through the power of the Great Library, it was possible for agents of change to travel between stories through any sort of door. Though it was possible to access these otherworldly doorways without Poe's help, (Dylan, in fact, often traveled without her aid.) Darke counted on her for guidance when his own fractured mind was uncertain of how to proceed.

Consulting the interface, however, he found it completely unresponsive…as if Poe had been shut down.

"What's wrong?"

"Nothing," Darke lied. "Follow me, please."

He had previously prepared a place for Evan Richmond to start his new life under the alias, Patrick Billings. There was a small frame house rented under that name with a year's worth of rent paid in advance. On the simple farm table inside its modest kitchen, a driver's license, birth certificate, social security card, and even falsified school records, waited to lend authenticity to "Patrick" and his new life.

Darke, however, didn't open a door into Evan's new home. His every instinct prompted him toward caution, so he opened a doorway into the tool and garden shed in the rental home's backyard. The small shack smelled of mulch and fertilizer, but it did nothing to cover the scent Darke had finally identified in Evan's cell. No sooner had the prisoner followed him through the door than Darke grabbed him by the shirt and pinned him to a shelving unit, sending bottles of motor oil and washer fluid tumbling to the ground.

Before the warrior could say anything, Evan smiled at him and asked, "What gave me away? I slipped up mentioning the necromancer, didn't I? I wasn't supposed to know he was 'The Eyes' that killed my friends, huh?"

"That was one slip up. The other was the smell," Darke said through clenched teeth. "I caught the scent of blood deep beneath an assortment of cleaning products. Not unusual for a hospital, even of the psychiatric variety, but then I noticed what I had missed upon entering."

"Do tell."

Darke found the young man's smile unsettling.

"Your roommate. At first, I thought he was merely sleeping in the corner. But amid the sea of noises, including our voices, I never once heard him breathing."

"Lanny was a snorer," Evan said without a hint of emotion. "If he was alive, we'd have both had trouble hearing each other. Plus, he'd have squealed like a piggy over me breaking loose."

"You aren't a murderer," Darke said, shaking him violently. "You're a victim!"

"Past tense! You and your boy changed all that! In fact, despite all your lies, you gave me a great gift."

His sneer prompted Darke to let go of him.

"You're mad!"

"No, I'm ringing clear as a bell, hero. This isn't madness. It's rage. It was the gift you gave me when you left me to rot. Hate and contempt…for you *and* your Author."

"The Author willed your rescue! Your story was never meant—"

"Liar!"

Darke felt the pruning shears slide into his belly before he realized the man he had come to set free had even grabbed them. He looked down to see blood spilling out onto Evan's hand as it twisted the makeshift weapon sharply. Suddenly unable to stand, Darke crashed against one wall of the shack, which broke away completely and landed with him in the sand of some unfamiliar island.

Blinded by the too-bright sun and trying to hold his insides together, he could not process what was happening.

"Why?"

"I was offered a better deal," Evan said. "I sat in that nut house for seven years. *Seven years!* You and your friend never showed. Seven years paying for something I didn't do. Something I was powerless to prevent. You and Dylan with all your power? Power *I* had been destined for, *b-t-dubs.* You did nothing! Didn't save my friends. Didn't save me. Just left me to fester at the funny farm while my potential, the life of adventure I might have had, was squandered."

"That isn't…Evan, your path diverged from the Author's intention *long* before that awful night in your apartment. In ways small and great, you chose to put yourself before others. You shunned the wealth of your parents in some attempt to prove your moral superiority, but generosity is about so much more than how you use your wealth. It's also about how you use your time. How you show compassion. How quick you are to forgive. But you…chose *yourself* over others time and again. The necromancer's interference didn't derail your destiny, Evan. You did."

"More lies. More manipulation. You act as if the world rewards selflessness, Darke, but it doesn't. You've got to put yourself first because you can be damn sure no one else will."

"That isn't true!"

"Of course, it is. You and your mini-me, Dylan? You're

suckers! The two of you go jumping into other worlds… other realities where you could be gods. And what do you do? Talk someone out of stepping off a bridge? Prevent a war? Rescue a kid from vampires? For what? What do you get from that?"

"We serve the will of the Author," Darke said softly, his head beginning to swim.

"Why? Have you been promised a happy ending? A white picket fence with the girl of your dreams? You're trading godhood for a Joe job, pal! And you can't even see that you're a loser."

"I'm no god, Evan. Neither are you. It is in our nature to love ourselves above all others, that much is true. We offer the pretense of unity, of love for our fellow man, so we might feel a bit better about ourselves. But we make terrible, jealous, and spiteful gods. The Author has called us to a higher service…and a greater love."

"Save it for Sunday, preacher. You may kowtow and deny yourself a shot at having it all, but not me. See, before ol' Dylan came to see me, I had *another* visitor," Evan said, "and she promised me that, if I could be patient, I would eventually get my chance for revenge. She'd give me all the power I need to write my *own* story. To be my own god. All she wanted in exchange was to get you out of the picture."

"Evan, that woman is lying to you. She doesn't have the authority to—"

"She told me all about you, Darke. When you'd come. How I could beat you. Even what a simp you are for your Big Boss. She told me she already had someone in place to take Dylan off the board, too. From what you said, it seems she was successful. Now, with *your* death, my part of the bargain is done."

Darke pulled the pruners from his abdomen and tossed them aside.

"She told me you'd be almost impossible to kill under most circumstances," Evan admitted, squatting beside him and digging his finger into Darke's wound, smiling broadly as the warrior screamed. "She said you were damn near invincible outside your own narrative. You don't seem so tough now, though."

Evan stood and walked back toward the shack, which Darke could now see was nothing but a façade…little more than a movie set situated in the middle of a beach. They certainly weren't in Iowa.

Picking up a sledgehammer from the debris of the shed, Evan proceeded to destroy it, blow after violent blow, until nothing remained of the structure but broken fragments. Out of breath, he staggered back to Darke and dropped to his knees in the sand.

"She hijacked your door, pal," he said with a laugh that bordered on maniacal. "Brought you inside your own narrative using this cool little orb she got her hands on. *Here* I could hurt you, she said. Here I could end you."

"Impossible!" Darke gasped, the pain in his gut making it hard to speak.

"Why? Because your boss said he'd protect you? He doesn't care about you, Darke, any more than he cares about me. He only cares about his story. You're just...a cog in the wheel. A tool to be used and then cast aside. My queen told me everything."

"Evan, she lies!"

"*You* lied! You promised you'd help me. Or your boy did. Either way, you both abandoned me. But she didn't. Came to me repeatedly throughout the years. She even took me to your Not-So-Great Library for a little research field trip. Preparing me. Getting me ready to join her. To become her Margrave."

"That woman, this so-called Queen, doesn't need you," Darke managed. "She's only telling you what you want to hear."

"You're right," Evan said, his smile twisted and profane. "She doesn't need me. She *wants* me. She wants me because it will wound him."

"Azael?"

"No. Not your wizard. The Author. She means to strike at his very heart."

"She's out of her depth. There is nowhere to run...nowhere to hide...that is so far away the Author cannot find you. It isn't too late, Evan. You can still turn from this folly and live."

Evan laughed at that until he was hoarse and coughed.

"Thanks for *that*. Been a while since I had a good laugh. She's already beaten you, Darke. *I've* beaten you. And now I'll let you die nice and slow. It'll hurt you know. Baking out here in the sun. Bleeding out into the sand. All your tattooed spells and protections won't save you here. We knew better than to attack you with magic. Not when a good old-fashioned stab wound would do the trick. Dylan is dead. You're not far behind him. And Azael, that pesky little magic man, will be next."

Darke wept. Not from pain and not from fear. His heart broke for the wounded man consumed by vengeance.

A portal opened beyond the wreckage of the fake shack. It seemed familiar to Darke, though he couldn't recall how.

"Time for me to *hasta*," Evan said, standing. "Don't speed death along by trying to get out of this, Cape Guy. I smashed the only door into bits. There's no means of escape. No rescue coming your way. Just death. Slow, painful, bloody death. Any last words you want me to deliver to Her Majesty?"

"Not for her. For you," Darke managed. "I forgive you, Evan."

"Gee, thanks," Evan replied with a sneer.

Darke watched as Evan stepped through the portal only

for it to close behind him. He whispered a prayer for the man who had betrayed him and for his missing charge, Dylan. Then, he asked for forgiveness. Somehow, he and his protégé had helped create a monster of their own.

"Help," he pled softly as darkness encroached the edges of his vision. "I still believe. Please...help me."

ACKNOWLEDGEMENTS

To Heidi: As with most things in my life, this work would not have been possible without your love, support, and encouragement. I am forever grateful that the Author saw fit to write you into my life...and me into yours.

To my children, B, Ember, and Jacob: Thanks for listening to my crazy ideas, for not being *too* impressed, and for filling my life with laughter and the best hugs any dad could hope for.

To Susie Mengelt, for the title inspiration. I'm sure Lee would be pleased by our collaboration.

To Bob Raymond: Thank you for all you've done on projects seen and unseen. That you don't get more work is criminal.

To Caitlin and Shawn at Mood Coffee Co. for giving me a home away from home...a place to create new worlds. You do your family and your community proud.

To my Patreon supporters: Your kindness and grace keeps me going. That you support me with your hard-earned money is humbling.

To you, Dear Reader, thank you for taking the time to read these scary little stories. Without you, none of this matters.

THREE MEN...
BOUND BY HOPE.

DYLAN,
THE WILLING.

AZAEL,
THE WIZARD.

DARKE,
THE WOUNDED.

WELCOME TO THE EVERMORE...
YOUR FREE NOVELLA AWAITS!

author photos by Shawn Crone

J. Patrick Lemarr lives in Indiana with his wife, Heidi, and their children. When he isn't crafting horror and fantasy, he is writing exclusive content for his Patreon supporters.

WWW.JPATRICKLEMARR.COM
WWW.PATREON.COM/JPATRICKLEMARR
WWW.FACEBOOK.COM/THEOFFICIALJPATRICKLEMARR
WWW.TWITTER.COM/JPATRICKLEMARR
WWW.YOUTUBE.COM/POPPOPFIZZLE
WWW.BUZZSPROUT.COM/1121975

www.ingramcontent.com/pod-product-compliance
Lightning Source LLC
Chambersburg PA
CBHW070728280626
47159CB00023B/2876